A Murd

Dick... ...y, well lit, so I spotted the three men a second before they rushed me. The blackjack stung my cheek as I threw myself backwards and rolled. A foot kicked my thigh as I jerked the thirty-eight from its resting place in the small of my back and fired onto the paving stones. They weren't gunboys and shied back. I heard the ricochet and one of them gave the convulsive twitch that everybody gives when a bullet hits them.

The leader was a vast, disorganized hulk of a man with a face pounded into vacancy. One of the other two was small, broad and piglike. The other was a thin, sallow youth with pimples.

For a split second we faced each other. Then someone muttered "Scram", and they rushed for the entrance to the alley. There, wearing his usual lop-sided, grimacing smile, was Gould, the Homicide man. His gun looked big in his hand. Blood started to ooze on to the sallow youth's yellow shoe.

I got up and frisked them for him. Apart from the leather-covered clubs they were clean. Presently the wagon came along and we watched them loaded in.

"No hurry," said Gould, "they'll be booked on sus. Better call down at the precinct house tomorrow and sign a complaint. And you owe me a drink."

Other titles in the Walker British Mystery Series

KENNETH
GILES

A Murderous Journey

WALKER AND COMPANY · NEW YORK

First published in the United States of America in 1975 by the
Walker Publishing Company, Inc.

This paperback edition first published in 1985.

ISBN: 0-8027-3125-2

Library of Congress Catalog Card Number: 75-4403

Printed in the United States of America

10   9   8   7   6   5   4   3   2   1

Sᴜɴᴅᴀʏ ᴛᴀꜱᴛᴇᴅ ʜᴏʀʀɪʙʟᴇ and there was a dentist's drill in my left ear. My eyes came stickily open. The May light streamed through the big window of my living-room, making the electric lights pallid and sickly. I'd gone to sleep on the big couch, a thing I'd sworn never to do again the last time I had it re-upholstered. The buzzing noise came from the telephone on a ledge above the couch.

I got to my feet and pain washed up into my skull. I made the bathroom and after a while got round to shaking a handful of effervescent salt on to a toothbrush. After a time the lumps disappeared from my mouth and teeth. I blundered back and my eyes focused on the plastic cards spilled among the sticky liquid rings on the table-top.

I cursed as my foot crunched broken glass. My old army buddy! "Piron, guess who's in town raring for action?" Bleared eyes focused on a bra dangling from one chair. I remembered we'd played strip poker with the girls. Weary footsteps took me to the bedroom door. I peeked. Empty. I thanked God and stood looking at the telephone, still buzzing remorselessly. I picked up the handset. It was the Boss, the Old Man, the Destiny who shapes the end of Piron, for one hundred and seventy bucks payable every Friday, expense sheets rigidly checked.

"Piron?"

"Yes." My voice sounded like rusty tins.

"You hung over?"

"Yes."

"I want you in the office at eight forty-five."

"It's Sunday."

"Piron, I can read. I've got a big calendar on my desk, remember?"

He hung up. I looked at my wrist-watch. It was ten

minutes after seven. I took four grains of aspirin, wallowed in a hot bath, shivered under a cold needle shower, forced myself to drink a pint of coffee and chew two pieces of toast with anchovy paste. I thanked God the apartment was serviced, and put down a two-buck tip for the old lady who did the cleaning.

I was comparatively human when I strode into the office lobby. We operate a switchboard on Sundays and a couple of other businesses keep a skeleton staff.

Everybody coming in has to sign a book. The names above mine were all familiar except one. "J. Brown, Roosevelt Hotel" was written in small, characterless writing. I shrugged and went into the Old Man's private office, next to the conference room, a heavily old-fashioned place where we hypnotise the wealthier prospects. As I opened the door I saw the client.

He was a tiny man, impeccably neat, with a round face like a smooth-skinned red apple. His eyes were yellowish, as though he suffered from jaundice, and he had the most unpleasant expression on his face that I reckoned I'd ever seen.

He sat at the Old Man's desk as though he owned it. The Old Man himself squatted in a corner chair, for once looking apprehensive.

"Piron," said the little man without troubling to greet me. "I want you to listen to me very carefully. I imagine this will be both the first and last conversation we will have. I gather you have a reputation as a wit and a wag. When I'm around, any wittiness or waggery comes from me, and that occurs very rarely."

He kept his eyes unwinkingly upon my face. Inwardly I said, "Kid stuff," but aloud I made a noise like "Yessir".

"Fine," he said. "I know your security rating and that you've worked with Security before. You also know New York better than most people. Now, eighteen months ago a truck smashed down a concrete post at the end of a bridge. The post was old and had cracks in it. When they started to clear up the debris, one of the workmen found a small metal capsule and gave it to the nearest cop. The police lab had a look at it. Inside was a roll of microfilm of a top-ranking document concerning our relations with Red China."

He paused to light a king-size cigarette which jutted out of his little mouth like a cannon aboard a dinghy.

"We got the man who photographed it. The usual story —he thought we were handling Red China incorrectly, so he decided to become a traitor. He shot himself before we could pick him up. In any case it would be a thousand to one against him knowing any names that mattered to us.

"Now you probably know all this, but I'll tell you all the same. Sometimes these spy rings work in small teams, generally three or four, of which one is a woman. The other method is the spymaster, who rarely contacts an agent personally. The routine is for the spymaster to locate a 'drop' for correspondence : maybe in the cistern of a public toilet, a hole in a fence post. Stuff like that. The agent is informed by post or telephone where his current 'drop' is. It's an old method but the best so far devised.

"Right. A few months afterwards we got a bonus from a neutral country. This time it was a typewritten report summarising the latest information the State Department had, or thought they had, about Red China's air strength. It was upsetting, to say the least. There are other indications that Chinese intelligence inside this country is operating as a separate unit on an increasing scale, independent of other communist countries. We don't like it.

"We took steps. The semantic experts said that the writer, although he or she spoke American fluently, was probably not educated here. They guessed perhaps southern Europe. The typewriter examiner said the machine was a Remington, ten years old, and that the typist was fluent, not profession-ally trained, and probably a man by the touch.

"I may say that we have checked every second-hand type-writer shop in the state without success, so presumably the writer still has his machine, which is a lead."

"Unless he works in a typewriter shop," I jabbed at him.

"What's that?"

"Had a case once," I said slowly, "where a guy who ran a second-hand typewriter joint used to type anonymous letters. Before he posted one, he made sure that particular machine had been sold, always to an out of state source."

He blinked his eyes. "That's a new one!" His voice was grudging. "To continue, we made the working hypothesis that the ring-leader would not be of Chinese descent. I know you get the pale-skinned, burly Chinese type, but a man with a yellow skin is still uncommon enough to make it dangerous for him to engage in espionage work. So, okay, it's a professional. Take a man who emigrated here, has sympathies with the communist system, and likes the money and power the work brings. Also a dangerous, ruthless man."

He paused and stubbed the cigarette, half smoked. "There was a newspaper man* around town named Harry Siskin. Did you know him?"

The name half-rang a bell. Finally I shook my head.

"Siskin was forty-seven. We picked him in 1944 for advanced intelligence. He was smart and a good patriotic man. After the war he majored in journalism on a government grant. At the same time my predecessor approached him to join the department. Harry said that he wanted to try journalism." He shook his head. "Oh, no nonsense about wanting to write plays or books—newspaper work attracted him. So we let him go and he worked on various papers all over the place. In 1953 he settled in New York. I'd taken over by then and I approached him. Our reports were that he was a better desk man than reporter. What he liked to do was to write special pieces—he was an authority on old New York and things like that. He made a fair living selling these specials and working a week-end shift for a Sunday sheet. He agreed to my proposal and he was an excellent front, with plenty of time for the half a dozen assignments I gave him each year. He dealt with me direct or one assistant and never once associated with another agent.

"By the time I assigned him to this case we'd picked up a few other clues. The man we were after was of considerable physical strength and probably lived in Manhattan.

Siskin worked on it for three months. He got nowhere, as happens in ninety per cent of the cases. Three months ago he was found in a hotel room in Spanish Harlem. He was sprawled on the bed, quite dead. On the washstand was a bottle of peach brandy. A glass had rolled out of his hand onto the floor; the stuff was laced with cyanide. The police and the coroner put it down as suicide. There was a piece of evidence that Harry was very depressed for a couple of days before his death."

He cleared his throat. "Of course, we kept right out of it. In the kind of agreement we had with Harry, the department arranges an insurance policy which takes care of retirement or provides a handsome sum in case of death. Therefore the widow was taken care of."

"Widow?" He'd made me jump in spite of myself.

He nodded. "Oh, yes, we vetted her carefully. She came out as an A.1 risk. Nevertheless Siskin never revealed to her his association with the department. She was fourteen years younger. You'll see her in," he glanced at his watch, seated clumsily on his slender wrist, "in about four minutes."

This time I kept dead-pan. The Old Man harumphed and said, "Yesterday afternoon Mrs. Siskin came in around four. She saw Jones and wanted us to take the case. He told her that it would be useless and that we don't ah, well, take that kind of case." Unless the client has a very long banking account, I thought.

"Then," the Old Man said, "I got a phone call from, ah, our friend here, the result of which was that I phoned her back, said that I'd decided to take the case and would she come in here at nine."

A buzzer rang on the desk. The Old Man arose ponderously and went to the wall, where he slid back an oak panel. One-way glass made a large peephole into the next room and the microphone relayed a slight, nervous, feminine cough. I stood back to let the apple-faced gentleman have first peek, and then, in order of seniority, the Old Man. She had twisted the client's chair sideways to avoid the morning light from the window and all I could see was the top of a mop of burnished, almost bronze hair. If it was naturally so, I guessed it spelled trouble. I know: I'm a red-head myself.

The little gentleman didn't turn his head as he said, "A daily report to Mr. Brown at the address you know."

We left him there.

The woman got to her feet as we entered. The first impression I had hit me right between the eyes. If Mrs. Siskin entered a room, people would look at her. Her skin was, like mine, of that matt white which goes with the hair. Green eyes looked sharply from under arched eyebrows, unfashionably thick.

Her voice was a trifle husky. "I'm Gretyl Siskin."

The Old Man has a kind of elephantine gallantry which goes down well with women. He patted the guest chair forward an inch.

"I spoke to you on the telephone, Mrs. Siskin. I'm sorry about yesterday. It so happens we're piled up with work, but I considered that we'd at least have a look at your case. You see," he gave that deep warm twisted smile of his, "we don't like piling up expense for people when there is no likelihood of results." He waved a hand towards me. "This is Mr. Piron who will do a preliminary look round."

I'd been studying her while he was speaking. Her personality had at first stifled the usual Piron—purely professional —survey. Now I saw that she was in the full ripeness of her beauty, about five feet five, long slim legs as a pedestal for hips with a promise of voluptuousness which was not negatived as my eyes went higher.

She glanced at me. Her vivid face lacked make-up. She'd put on a yellow skirt and an old sweater. Her shoes were flat. I wondered whether she was usually a careless dresser. I hoped not.

"When your man said 'no' I didn't trouble to try elsewhere. I went home, got out the record player and a bottle of whisky, and locked the door. Your man said I was hysterical. I wasn't."

I couldn't imagine her being hysterical.

"All right, Mrs. Siskin, just tell us the story. Piron will take notes." I got out notebook and pencil and let her talk. Actually her words would be recorded on tape, but clients like the sight of a man with a notebook.

She was thirty-four. (Dressed up she'd look eight years younger.) Her maiden name was Price. She'd been married before, unhappily, to a man named Scott who had got drunk one night and driven his car off the road and killed himself. She had met Harry Siskin five years ago in Denver, two years after Scott's death. Four years ago she and Siskin were married. No children by either marriage.

Her low, husky voice paused. I wondered if she had rehearsed her speech.

The Old Man said, "If you'll excuse me, you make a workmanlike job of giving the facts."

A faint smile crossed her face like the wind rustling a bed of flowers. "I was a newspaper reporter. Oh, not big time, but I learned conciseness sweating away at dull court reporting. When Scott died I'd gone back to it. As I say, Harry kept having to chase down to Denver to see me, so finally he said the plane fares were getting too much, so I'd better marry him and move into the apartment he'd taken here." A faint reminiscent dimple of pleasure popped into her left cheek.

"Keep me to the point if you want. I'm trying to give you a picture of Harry. He was a big man physically, very gentle and slow-spoken. Life with him went very quickly. There were so many things we'd planned to do—children, maybe a trip to Europe. He had a great sense of humour. Financially, we had just enough. He worked week-ends on a paper, and sold quite a lot of feature stuff. He liked poking around the city and knew a great deal about it. His delight was finding old characters who'd lived all their life here. In fact his ambition was to do a series of books on New York from 1840 until now. Harry wasn't a brilliant writer. He was a great man on facts and research, careful and patient, but writing came hard to him and if he attempted what we call colour stuff it came out flat. On the other hand, I'm quite good at it, so we collaborated a good deal."

She thought for a few seconds. "What I'm trying to project is that Harry wasn't an aggressive, nosy, scandal-digging type of newspaperman. I guess he'd never consciously seen a gangster. He liked helping people and I don't think he had many enemies."

"He had some?" I asked.

She fumbled in a small briefcase, produced a thick envelope. "I wrote down there everything I could remember about Harry's personal relationships, with a summary of his business affairs. There's a few photographs of him, too . . ." Her voice trailed away and her eyes became moist. I reached over and took the envelope.

"How were you left financially?" The Old Man's voice was suitably funereal.

She gestured. "I told the other man I was comfortably fixed. We had a joint life policy for eight thousand dollars, but unknown to me he'd carried a much bigger one. I got seventy-five thousand dollars after taxes."

"You knew nothing of this other policy?"

"It wasn't like Harry not to tell me, but like him to think of me. I hate to think of him cutting down on meals out, things like that, to pay the premiums. When . . . when the police came, I told them of the policy I knew about." She hesitated and I watched her intently out of the corners of my eyes. "Then this other company wrote me, and after I checked it wasn't a mistake I told the police. I think," she hesitated again, "I think that if I hadn't had an iron-clad alibi I'd have had a rough time. I've done enough around the courts to know that I'd be number one suspect. As it happened, a girl friend from Chicago was a house-guest. We hadn't seen each other for two years, but we're pretty close. We'd spent the day together at her aunt's hotel apartment."

The Old Man asked her would she mind if he lit a cigar and while he was fumbling with the cutter I had time to think. A surprisingly high proportion of well-to-do murderers hire private richards to delve into the demise of the victim.

There is a two-fold motive. One is that if they do find them-selves before a jury, the high-price counsel can make great play about "my client's unremitting efforts to unveil her dear husband's killer". Second, they guess that the agency reports may reveal exactly how much the cops have found out to date.

"That day," she said, her voice flat, "was January 20th, a Saturday. There's a dirty little hotel in Spanish Harlem called Pablo's. Pablo's Palace, the locals call it. It's a few steps up from a flop-house. They don't allow women there. The rooms are all single. You go into a dirty little reception hall and there's two old drive-yourself elevators. I guess the place has twenty-five rooms. The people are mostly seedy-looking: old suits carefully pressed every couple of days. A lot of horse players live there. Everybody's got some get-rich-without-working angle and they are so absorbed in it they don't notice anybody outside their private dream. Can I have a cigarette, please?" I went over with a case. As I lit it I could smell the faint, sweet perfume of good toilet soap.

"Now this place," she said, "has got an old guy behind the desk who's a wino. The owner comes in once a day to collect the rents—it is strictly no credit. He's a big, tough, oldish man called Johnny Henlo. The old clerk has just got sufficient brain to give you a key and push the register forward and take a night's money if you're a man. He thought my husband booked in without luggage, which isn't uncommon—most of the clients carry a clean shirt and a toothbrush in a briefcase—at around one in the afternoon.

"The people there are mostly late risers and the three cleaners have difficulty sometimes. The owner's wife, Mrs. Henlo, who's a tough old lady indeed, always goes round between four o'clock and five o'clock and personally looks into each room. She never varies, and uses a passkey if the door is locked. When she looked into room 206 my husband was dead on the bed. The coroner's report is in that folder which you have. Against 206 in the register was scrawled 'Fred Smith', in what looked like my husband's writing.

"That's about all," she said. "He'd been dead around an hour. They told me he couldn't have suffered much." Her voice was bitter. "It was cyanide in peach brandy. Verdict, suicide."

"One thing," I said. "Your husband's drinking habits."

"My first husband was a drunk. It ran in his family and was compulsive. Harry liked a drink and could take it or leave it. When he had his sessions with the old-timers he'd mull, as he used to say, over a stein of beer. But he'd often take a couple of drinks during the day, and he did like to try out-of-the-way stuff. The bar at home has maybe two dozen bottles of liqueurs I'd given him for birthdays and celebrations. They're all three-quarters full. He'd have a small measure when he was in the mood."

She stubbed the cigarette, and suddenly looked very tired.

"Was your husband normal in manner the week he died?" asked the Old Man.

She looked mad. "Those idiots of policemen said that the other men where he worked said not. He used to start work on the Sunday magazine supplement at eight o'clock on Friday morning. He'd get home around eight that night. Then, on Saturdays, he'd get up at six to get into the office and quit at noon. In the afternoons he'd have a few drinks with the boys he worked with and usually got home around five. That day he said he'd be late and I wasn't to save dinner."

"So you didn't see much of him on the Friday and on Saturday morning."

She said, with a kind of little-girl pride, "I always got up and gave him breakfast. You see, we had a house-guest and I had a lot of things to talk to her about. On Friday night Harry sipped a couple of Scotches and mostly listened. If he *was* worried he would be too polite to reveal it in front of a guest. We went to bed around ten-thirty. He went straight to sleep and I read for a bit."

"And on Saturday morning?"

A patch of colour crept into her cheeks. Her long legs shifted uneasily.

"I didn't tell the police this. Louise, my girl friend, wasn't out of the bath. He'd picked at his breakfast and when he got up to go I said, for no conscious reason, 'Is everything okay, Harry?' He put his arms round my hips, swung me into the air, and said, 'Everything is just fine, Popsy.'" Her eyes misted again. "It sounds silly cold, but he said it slowly in his deep voice."

"Ah, well," the Old Man said. "Leave it to us for a couple of days, Mrs. Siskin. My suggestion is that you make out a cheque to us for five hundred dollars. We'll put that amount of work into it and see how we go."

"I'd rather have five thousand dollars' worth of work," she said, getting up.

He smiled and shook his head. "Mrs. Siskin, we know what we are doing. We've a reputation as an agency to maintain."

"Oh, I know. You're very kind." She went to the little table and took out her cheque-book. Over her shoulder she said, "I suppose the police will co-operate with you. I mean, should I tell them you are representing me?"

I saw the Old Man's eyebrows twist. "No," he said casually, "that won't be necessary. I guess they will let us have a look through the folder."

He took the cheque from her and shook her hand. She turned to me, and her handclasp was firm, but not too firm. I dislike women who try to shake hands like a man. The eyes looked up at me. She turned on the sex appeal, "I know you'll do your very best, Mr. Piron."

When she'd gone I looked at the Old Man and raised my eyebrows. He chewed his cigar and raised his in return.

I summed up. "Personality plus and dominant. Knows how to use her appeal if it helps. Brains. I didn't like that casual mention of the cops."

We've been together long enough not to waste words.

"Women like that are either very good or very bad," he said. "She reminds me of an aunt of mine. She bullied the

soulcase out of mayors, ministers and up to the Governor—
and all for slum clearance in the bad old days. She had two
thousand people at her funeral."

"Do you remember the lady from Dallas?" I grunted.

He did, we all did. She'd had enough charm and personality to float a boat and steam-rollered her way through life.
She wasn't quite quick enough in cremating her old aunt,
who was practically embalmed in arsenic.

"We'll see," he said. We went back to his office. Our little
visitor had gone. The Old Man slid back the panel over
the peep-hole.

I went over to Homicide Headquarters and had a word
with a detective named Dickens. He's an old friend and
suffers under the cross of a Christian name of Charles, which
has branded him among Headquarters wits as Nickle-ass
Nickleby.

He butted his cigarette in a rusty tin can beside his
typewriter. "I laugh, Piron, to see private dicks working on
Sunday along with public ones. Your boss phoned mine.
Sure, you can see the folder; it's dead as the fish I ate last
night in a crummy Greek joint. He committed suicide. If
he didn't, your client wrapped him up."

He pounded away on a report about the Greek, who,
besides selling fish, was suspected of killing his son-in-law.
I read and studied the photographs. Harry Siskin's face
wasn't pleasant in the morgue shots.

As I read I got the impression that if the cops had known
about the big insurance policy at the start they might have
conducted the case a different way. As it was, they'd
thought it was suicide from the start. Only Siskin's prints
were on the glass and bottle. They hadn't traced the
source : the brandy was a good imported Polish variety, not
so uncommon that any upper-bracket store wouldn't carry
it. Two men who worked with Harry on the Sunday supplement said he was tense, withdrawn and even snappy, quite
unlike his usual self. He'd said to another guy he'd met
on the Thursday, "I'm about to resign from the human
race, I guess." It's the usual cliché, the thing a man says

when his wife has complained about his drinking, the boss has double-crossed him on a raise, or there's been another nuclear explosion. But it was unlike Harry to say it.

The cops had clung to that thought. The hotel was a dead lead. Nobody could remember any caller for Harry. As long as it wasn't a woman, the old clerk, who was half blind from cheap alcohol, never stopped anybody using the lift. Most of the guys in the place used their rooms for business as well as sleeping.

As to Gretyl Siskin, the evidence was conclusive in one way. Her house-guest was a Mrs. Kramer from Chicago. They had both spent the day with a Kramer aunt, a half-senile old lady who still made a nuisance of herself in a suite in a once very fashionable hotel not far from Times Square. Both Mrs. Kramer and her aunt by marriage swore that Gretyl had been with them from eleven in the morning until four, when Mrs. Kramer and Gretyl took a taxi back home.

The trouble is that once a witness says as much, you can never make him budge. Had the police originally suspected homicide their approach would have been oblique. "Do you remember exactly how long Mrs. Siskin took in the ladies' room?" "Do you remember Mrs. Siskin going to the desk for cigarettes?"

On the time factor Gretyl might have got to the hotel and back in thirty minutes. When people say, "He or she was with me all day," they forget the little interludes, and Gretyl was a smart woman.

I could think of dozens of ways it might have happened. Women were not allowed into the hotel, but was the rule rigidly enforced? I'd have guaranteed that there were ways of getting a woman into the place.

For a guy who combined being an undercover agent with journalism, both professions that are kind to butterflies in the stomach, Harry Siskin sounded pretty calm. I've known guys who never drank much, but occasionally took a bottle to some out-of-the-way hotel room and drank the lot. Gretyl might have provided Harry's last bottle.

By the time the police knew of the big insurance cover, they'd about closed the file. The man handling it, a fellow named Gould, wasn't too happy. He'd seen the insurance company who had guardedly said that "to the best of their knowledge" Gretyl hadn't known about the policy. I read his summation of the case. If you knew police work it meant that the case was dead, but the man in charge wasn't too happy.

"Nickle-ass," I said, "is Gould around?"

He grunted and looked down the long room as he took the file back, "Sure," he said, "come along."

He introduced me to a thin, rumpled-looking man.

"Make it Tuesday, Piron," said Gould twisting his mouth in a grimace. "I've put in a seventy-hour week and I spent last night on my feet."

"There's a restaurant near here that opens Sunday and specialises in three-inch steaks and I'm on expenses."

"You're on," he said, "as long as it's strictly your account. But I warn you, my brains are addled."

I waited until maybe three-quarters of a pound of steak, with mushrooms, french fried and cream gravy, was in him. He took another pull out of the silver tankard of strong beer and slumped back in his seat.

"Okay, Piron, that saved my life. If this is private detecting, I'm looking at the Help Wanted ads. Now, the Siskin case. Suicide? All the time I worked on it my neck prickled. When my neck prickles it means something wrong."

He finished the steak and mopped the plate with bread.

"Siskin wasn't the kind of journalist who gets acid thrown in his face. Quiet, friendly kind of big man everybody liked. That left the wife. Take her. Nothing I'd like better than taking her for a quiet week-end. If I didn't have a wife, two kids and exhaustion from over-work. She pestered the life out of us until finally I wouldn't see her. Then she got to the lieutenant twice before he put the bar up."

"So she goes to us," I said. "I read your report and smelled you didn't like it."

"Gretyl Siskin," he said slowly. "First husband a no-good.

The newspapers she worked for say she was the crusading type: ill-treatment of animals, vivisection, poor old ladies in homes getting slapped by brutal nurses. Good white-hot prose. Only, they always had to recheck. Her indignation was often stronger than her facts. A do-gooder, in fact."

"Boy friends?"

"I put a woman on the job, gal with ears like antennae. She struck the delicatessen stores near where Gretyl lives. If any guy knows the scandal, it's the grocer. No soap. Lovely Mrs. Siskin. The same with the beauty parlour."

"Alibi?"

He shrugged. "There was a time when the senile old aunt and the girl friend were in the downstairs restaurant with Gretyl. The old lady had forgotten her wallet—they'd had lunch and were sipping coffee. Gretyl went to get it. The girl friend was gabbing away trying to consolidate with her husband's wealthy auntie. How long Gretyl was away is anyone's guess."

He took time to order apple pie with whipped cream.

When he was half-way through the pie I said, "Did Harry Siskin make a practice of shacking up in a cheap hotel with a bottle?"

His wise cop's face looked at me. "I thought of that. The guy knew this city better than most. If he did he'd never take the same room twice. I thought of his wife planting the bottle and Harry taking it for a junket. If so, how the hell do you prove it?"

His jaws worked steadily for a while. "I'll give you a bonus for the pie, Piron. One thing didn't go into the report. The lieut. doesn't like what he calls extraneous bits. Siskin told his wife he worked every week on that Sunday sheet. He was lying. They've got a roster of a dozen men. In practice the guy in charge calls them up and asks if they are free. The average is two calls a month. And a few times Siskin used to turn the offer down, at that."

I wondered whether those were the occasions that Siskin worked for Mr. Brown. We drank our coffee in silence while the tiredness drained out of him. I collected the check and thanked him.

His long arm reached out and pulled me back into my seat.

"Piron," he said, "we keep sufficient tab on the agencies to know how they are doing. Your rathole is doing extra well currently. How come you took this on?"

His light brown eyes were very hard.

"She's got money."

He wagged his head. "Not for this kind of thing. Your agency doesn't throw its lousy ethics out of the window unless the client's an insurance company, a bank, or a guy who has got a couple of million bucks, in cash at that."

I leered at him. "A whim, Gould. We private richards are full of whims."

He let go of my collar. "Whim seizes me, Piron. To take out that dead file and work it. If the lieutenant won't give me time, I'll use my own."

"And the best of luck to ye," I said as I headed towards the cashier.

"Anything?" asked the Old Man, who was studying a trial balance sheet with some satisfaction when I got back.

"Could be the woman. The detective in charge is named Gould. He's taking the file out on account of he thinks you have ethics below a couple of million bucks."

He didn't flinch, merely screwed up his wrinkles into his eyebrows. The cigar smouldered in the big ashtray.

"The man in here this morning, Piron, let's call him Mr. Brown. He thinks it's easier to catch a murderer than a first-class spy. If the two are the same and Siskin was murdered, it's the biggest lead on the espionage."

He sighed and looked at the ceiling. At one time the Old Man handled quite a deal of Government business. It has been getting less mainly because there is almost a surplus among the great body of official anti-spy boys.

"Now," he said, "what Brown has in his evil little, but I assure you very fast-moving brain, is that we smoke the murderer out. If Gould puts in his ten cents, all the better.

It is forbidden, period, forbidden to give the police the slightest idea of what it's about."

I sat and thought while he produced a bottle of Scotch and poured two measures.

"You might say," he said, "that there is a difference between political and private assassination. In the political sphere it's anybody's guess how many agents get themselves knocked off each year. These guys are experts. But because Harry Siskin's life slopped over into the civil area, so did the crime. And that's the weakness."

"So we get the murderer, and the little guy takes over."

He nodded. I added, "And tells him he won't be prosecuted for murder if he opens right up."

Some, not a lot, of the Official Attitude has rubbed off on to the Old Man. He gulped the rest of his whisky and I knew he was hornet-mad. His eyes were very cold.

"Piron," he said, "sometimes I wonder how soon it will be that somebody holes that Irish skull you keep poking out. If we solve this case we take our bonus from Mr. Brown and button our lips."

I stretched out the privileged hand of an old servant and helped myself to more whisky.

He pretended to study the balance sheet. I sat and thought.

"So she's the goat," I said at last.

He sneered slightly. "You took a long time to get to it. Yes, Mrs. Siskin is the tethered goat, if the theory is right."

I said it aloud, to annoy him. "So we make loud enough noise until Siskin's murderer, off the territory he knows, decides to fake a suicide for Gretyl, complete with confession note."

He just nodded.

"You should keep a spittoon around this office," I said, fighting mad.

He gave his split-faced grin. "Piron," he said, "Mr. Brown is an astute man. Two months ago the janitor who attends the apartments where Mrs. Siskin lives was offered a better job. By coincidence an unemployed janitor with impeccable references and a childish attitude about money had applied to the agents for a job. He is unmarried, but has two impeccable brothers who live with him in the janitor's apartment. And, the public purse being as deep as it is, a radio van keeps Mrs. Siskin in sight when she goes out."

I sighed. You can't win against the Old Man.

"Back to my desk and duty, sir," I said.

"Just one thing," he said as I reached the door. "Did you note the fair Gretyl's attitude to money? How the hell could the late lamented keep up that amount of insurance on lunch money? And when you see his apartment, work out how a man in his line of business could afford it."

"Maybe she didn't know what he was supposed to earn."

"And her experience in the same line of business?"

I meekly went into my cubby-hole and worked through the dossier Gretyl had left. She'd been thorough. The neat typing took me back through Harry Siskin's life, as she knew it. She must have written fifteen thousand words. By the time I'd finished I knew that Harry had a scar on his left shin he got from rescuing another schoolkid who'd got caught on a ledge down a quarry and couldn't get up. I knew he was the son of an unsuccessful lawyer, had been working through the University of South Illinois when war came, and had vegetarian leanings. I studied the photographs. A big man, maybe six feet three, with no surplus fat and a broad, gentle face except for a nose slightly mashed from football.

She had copied out his telephone notebook, plus the names of eighty-six people she remembered him knowing or doing business with. Two were starred.

They read thus :

James Bodleigh, 47, used to live in an apartment near ours, but moved away. Is an industrial chemist. (Old fellow pupil—the boy Harry rescued from the quarry.) A neurotic. Met Harry again after many years. Harry put a little money into an invention of Bodleigh's. He never got it back. Bodleigh claimed his invention was stolen and that Harry was involved. A plain lie. One day he came round with a wild look and attacked Harry. He's a little man and Harry just picked him up bodily and put him out the door the way you would a cat. Soon after he moved away.

John Marcello. I don't know the address but he's a big bookmaker. He came in one day in a rage—a big oily man with little black eyes that shift around. He used filthy words and accused Harry of playing around with Gwenda (his wife, I guessed). Harry told me that he'd done a bit of a line with her for a friend who wanted information for a story. One night when Harry was home Marcello came back with two thugs. Marcello started using bad language and Harry just got up and knocked one of the thugs down. He told M., "Keep on using that language and I do the same to you". M. quietened down and Harry told him that he had no interest in Gwenda whatsoever. Finally M. said, "Thass all right, thass all right," and went away with the bodyguards.

I red-ringed Marcello's name. I had heard of him vaguely as a nasty no-good with a big betting connection, and hence at least one foot in the shadows, the way it goes. Gwenda was the real name of a girl called Merlina. She was all curves, teeth and a smile that made strong men perspire, and worked the night clubs in a double dancing act. She changed partners often and the whisper was that Marcello wouldn't let her engage one who preferred women. He'd been stuck on her for the past three years, so much so that he still had to allow her to provide the nightly treats for nightclub patrons which she insisted on doing.

It was alleged that a few guys who didn't know the score had been roughed up for making passes at Gwenda. Murder? I didn't know.

I wrote a brief note, unaddressed and unsigned: "Have

you information re James Bodleigh (47) and John Marcello? Also what were Siskin's drinking habits?"

I asked the Old Man to get the note to Mr. Brown and took a cab out to Spanish Harlem. Sunday: best clothes: pointed toe-caps: girls in pairs: for once a fresh smell of late spring air mixed with other smells. The man who owned Pablo's Palace lived in a big old apartment. It was scrupulously clean, the furniture was old and solid, there was a pleasant smell of cooking. It had the atmosphere which comes from years of comfortable living.

The man I had come to see took me into a room where a woman sat in an old-fashioned chair with high sides to it. She was a big woman, her broad beam fitting comfortably to the wide seat. Hard work and energy had sweated the flesh off her face so you could see the big bones under the lined skin. She had snapping black eyes and white, carefully waved hair. I thought she might be seventy. With her type you have to see a certificate to be sure.

The owner had let me in himself. Johnny Henlo was a short squat hard man, completely bald, and with a mashed nose. His voice was pure New York. He glanced towards the woman.

"Mr. Piron, Mrs. Henlo."

The woman's head nodded very slightly. She kept her eyes on her husband.

"What gives that a private d. calls on me?" asked Henlo.

"You own the Pablo Hotel. A guy named Siskin got killed there."

He looked at his wife. Maybe it was telepathy, or muscle reading, or perhaps they'd worked together so many years that they automatically thought the same.

He turned his head and shrugged. "No dice, Mr. Piron."

Very slowly I picked my words. "Don't get into something you don't know about, Henlo. No co-operation and there's bad trouble for you. Fire-department trouble, income-tax trouble, for a start."

They looked at each other for fully half a minute. Then

he said, "A two-bit newspaperman means that trouble? Pfui!"

"It means that trouble," I said.

This time I thought I saw a slight pursing of Mrs. Henlo's lips.

"Okay," said Henlo. "I co-operate. And when Johnny Henlo says he won't co-operate, he doesn't give one per cent. But when he says he does, it's a hundred cents to the dollar. You ask around this place."

I pulled over a heavy mahogany chair with spindly legs and sat astride it.

"You own the Pablo joint, for a start?"

"It ain't no joint, mister." He stretched a big-palmed hand towards me. "Don't get that idea. I got eight hotels and none of 'em's crummy. I bought the Pablo ten years ago. It was a bad house—I'm sorry, Mother," he added, inclining his head to the old lady, who might have been carved out of stone.

"You know what, mister, Mother and me we vacationed one year down Florida. Big place with two swimming pools. I say to the proprietor, what percentage of vacancies you average? He said in the operating season he gets less than four per cent. Mister, I wiped the smile off his face. I said my eight places don't have point one per cent vacancies. And that's the year round."

I let him talk. When he did so his broad, swarthily impassive face achieved animation. I guessed he might be half Mexican. He'd always made a living running cheap rooming-houses. Twenty years ago he'd got the idea of very cheap hotels, a cut above the flop-house, for the guys who were still a cut above flop-houses. He had a couple of sons-in-law who looked after the other seven, but Pablo's he looked after himself.

"I told you what it was when I took over," he said. "The cops are threatening to put a lock on it. So I see the police and they say fine. But they warn me the place has a demolish order on it for slum clearance."

He looked at me with his wise old eyes. "Hell, you

know, mister, I been buying property in this city maybe forty years. I never had no building with a demolish order on it demolished." As he roared with laughter I saw his pink gums. His wife's face remained quite impassive.

The people who lived at Pablo's nearly all paid daily. As the majority of them were up late, the cleaning women didn't start to operate until ten thirty and finished two hours later. Mrs. Henlo personally went round inspecting the rooms every day at four. If something wanted doing she did it.

Except for the few permanents, the denizens of Pablo's carried their spare shirt and socks around with them. At six Henlo went round and waited for two hours. First preference went to regulars. They paid their money and got rights to one of the plaster boxes until next midday. By eight the place was filled and Henlo handed over to a tough local kid who'd fought prelims for a while. The nightman hung around until two a.m. when he left, after closing the front door.

I gave him a cigarette and lit up myself. If Siskin had booked in at one in the afternoon, as the rummy clerk thought, it would be the ideal time to get into the place unnoticed.

"Get many men booking in during the day?"

"Only a few," Henlo said. "Old Sam on the desk has got just enough sense to take the dough and make 'em sign the register. Most of the clients have to scuttle about all day promoting a little cash."

"I know you've got that no-women rule, Mr. Henlo. Now, on the level, can that rule be broken?"

He looked shocked, or tried to. Then he chuckled. "Ai, the things a man will do for a woman. Once or twice you get a guy trying. There's a back stair and a door leading out the other side of the block. The Fire Rules say it should be kept open. Pfui! A couple of times somebody tips the nightman some guy has a broad in his room and he chucks them both out. You see," he gave a solicitous leer at the immobile face of his wife, "excuse me, Mother, but the walls are pretty thin. Another roomer hears and he gets jealous, so he tips off the nightman."

"So you can get in the back door?"

"Not now. Fire Department or not, I put a big lock on and keep the key."

"You talk too much, Johnny." The old woman's voice was like the scraping of a file.

"Look, Mother, Mr. Piron's a gentleman. I co-operate a hundred per cent and there's no trouble for old Henlo. That right?"

"Sure as hell," I said. "Mind showing me the place, Mr. Henlo?"

I glanced at my watch. It was a quarter to four.

"Sure. It's time for Mother to go down there anyhow."

We went down to the street. Henlo and I walked ahead. The old lady stalked a few paces behind, lifting her feet high. I wondered if she had Indian blood in her.

Henlo and I walked past the hotel and she went in. He took me to the back of the block and into a crowded, broken street of tenement houses, which at this hour overspilled their tenants on to the sidewalk. I was conscious of curious, slightly hostile eyes, Henlo walked with stolid indifference until we came to a stout-looking iron-bound door.

"See! There's the lock."

I looked at it. It was the kind of lock that a person who watches the pennies buys, a big imposing-looking lock with lots of cheap metal. A lock that an educated child could open in maybe sixteen seconds. He inserted the heavy key and we entered the atmosphere of old crumbling plaster and carbolic that belonged to Pablo's Palace.

The back stairs were in good shape, but steep. I admired Henlo's agility as he bounced up ahead. We went up to the second floor, the last place Harry Siskin had seen on earth. The old man switched on the lights, which were a degree brighter than the amperage I associated with such places. The long corridor was cleanly painted, although the smell of old age and disinfectant was pervasive.

Henlo threw open the first door. It opened on to a twelve-by-eight box.

I looked and said, "You've made a good job of this," and meant it.

The customers got a room painted with a dark shade of plastic paint. A twelve-inch border of laminated wood ran round the wall bottoms to guard against clumsy feet. The bed was built in, and at the end was a little fixed table, with two small chairs. A washbowl big enough to bathe a small kitten faced the head of the bed. I tried the hot tap and the water was warm. A small piece of indestructible-looking burgundy-coloured carpet, an outsize ashtray on the floor, and a tiny closet with one hanger firmly fixed to a rod, completed the deal. I tapped a wall: it was thin plaster over the laths.

"Where's the room in which Siskin died?"

I followed him to the extreme end of the corridor. With pride he opened a door. It contained two shower stalls and two toilets. "Same on each floor," he said.

Room 206 was on the other side of the sanitary unit. It was the same as the other, but a trifle larger and had a large window. As I looked about I realised that it and the lavatory had originally formed one unit. I tapped the false dividing wall. It was solid against my knuckled fist.

"Mr. Henlo, would you please talk?"

He looked at me.

"Recite, sing, just anything!"

He looked embarrassed and started off "twice six are twelve", as I shut the door and went into the lavatory. I pressed my ear against the wall. I couldn't hear a thing.

I went back before he had got up to six eights and said I'd seen all I wanted. By that time the fever to co-operate had bitten him so that he was disappointed I didn't want to inspect every room.

The elevator was almost opposite, a creaky push-button affair. We got down into the small lobby, brightly painted and with a couple of pot plants flanking the tiny desk. A rheumy-eyed little old guy was half asleep behind.

A thought struck me. "Can I borrow your old registers, say over a two-year period?"

Nothing was too good for Piron and he produced six greasy books and wrapped them in newspaper.

I returned his handshake.

"And no trouble for Johnny, huh?"

"No, Johnny," I said.

It had turned warm and muggy, and there was no cab in sight. I cursed and walked along with the books under my arm.

"Homework?"

I side-stepped and saw the long lantern jaws and weary, cynical smile. It was Gould, the Homicide dick.

"I thought you were slated for around ten hours' sleep?"

He shrugged as he fell into step beside me. "One hour's sleep, a cold shower, and an understanding gal for a wife." I felt his eyes go down to the books.

"Old Henlo's registers, huh? That's an offence, buddy. He must keep them available for inspection at all times unquote."

"You on the licensing squad now, Gould?"

"Not now. I was for a time. Most guys stick to one detail for preference. I moved around. I'm the ambitious type and I learn. Such things as checking the back locks to superior fleapits."

He gave me a small, contemptuous smile. "Yeah, I had the lock taken off and looked at in the lab. Kid stuff. No scratch marks on the tumblers, no deposits of soft metal." The sudden change of pace seemed a favourite gambit with him. Abruptly he said, "And so what do you want with those registers?"

"Thoroughness, Friend Gould. Just routine. I want a handwriting expert to go through those books and try to see if Siskin registered more than once."

His long thin hand scratched at his nose and then massaged the faint fair stubble along his chin.

"I didn't do that. No point to it that I could see. It's

interesting that you're interested, if you follow me." I followed him and made a mental note to check on him.

I saw a taxi and hailed it with relief. He put a detaining hand on my arm and leaned his face close. His breath was a trifle bad.

"Piron, I saw the lieutenant and got him interested. If I put some spare time in on the Siskin file, he'll give me a couple of hours a day Squad time."

"Fine!" I brushed off his hand and got into the cab.

In the office I looked up the entry Siskin had made. "Room 206, Fred Smith, Baltimore." The writing was in red ball-point and angular. It still had character, which that kind of pen militates against. I pencilled a ring round it. I knew just enough to tell that it had been written in a hurry. It looked a well-practised kind of signature. I scribbled a note to the expert we employ and gave the messenger boy car fare. Then I called it a day.

Back home, I sat on the carefully smoothed couch and surveyed the uncluttered room, smelling the tang of furniture polish. It looked empty. Bachelor apartments do. The ladies, bless 'em, make fluffy, homely little single nests just so that a bachelor can contrast it with his own bleak quarters. I felt depressed and went to look in the liquor cabinet. As empty as my stomach felt. I cursed my dear old Army buddy, now, I prayed, safely back in Seattle.

Wondering whether it was worth phoning out for a supply, I reached for the handset, and on impulse phoned a contact I had.

"Is Marcello, the bookie, in town?"

"Hell, no. He's at a conference in Las Vegas, big deal."

"'With whom, about what?"

"A couple of bishops, a knotty problem in theology."

He prided himself on his waggery. I sighed into the phone. "'Okay, Len, then perhaps you know if his girl's around."

He laughed. "She's around, friend, but, say, aren't you getting ideas above your station, Piron?"

I hung up. I could feel the nasty little idea in my mind

growing bigger. I cautioned myself and found it didn't work.

The first social call was on a theatrical agent I knew. He came to the door in rumpled red pyjamas.

"Fine, Piron," he said. "I've just come to and was planning a drink." His big beefy face matched what he was wearing.

He slopped along the passage and towards the living-room bar. I took a straight rye.

"Haven't seen you for a year," he said.

We prattled lightly of this and that until I said, "A favour, Cy. Small favour. I want some oil on the beauteous Merlina."

He choked a bit over his drink. "I don't book her. She works steady and doesn't use an agent."

"A little oil," I begged.

"Hell, Piron, you must know about her and Marcello. You looking for a hole in the head?"

He poured himself another brandy and enveloped salted pretzels in one pudgy hand. His eyes surveyed me shrewdly as he thought.

"It's like this, Piron, and I'm putting it on the table. If you get yourself hock-deep in trouble, don't blame me. I got married again since I saw you. Girl's named Belinda. She sure as hell hates Merlina, though I never got it straight why it's that way."

I refilled my own glass, a very light helping. "Sounds promising, Cy. Where's Belinda?"

"That's just it. A hell of a thing. She flounced out of the flat three hours ago. Always does it. Walks about whipping her temper up and comes back. She's due any minute." His shrewd little eyes surveyed me craftily. "Get the point? If she thinks she can put Merlina in bad, why then, she forgets she's mad at me."

We changed the subject until we heard the noise of the front door being opened. I saw Cy tense.

"Cy! Cy!" The voice had the good old cutting edge to it. "I might have known you'd be at the bar. Oh!"

She saw me, I saw her. Petite, brunette, very beautiful if you liked a hint of plumpness. A good face, too, if it hadn't worn a fire-and-brimstone mask.

"This is Mr. Piron, honey, a private detective pal of mine."

"Divorce?"

"Occasionally."

"Then I could use you." She cimbed onto a bar stool, reached over and opened a soft drink.

"Honey," Cy placated, "he's after dirt on Merlina."

"That permanent bitch!"

Cy worked for a while, and presently I was getting the ears filled with Merlina. It was a complicated sort of thing, involving dressing-rooms and a stage manager. It took some time and got so that I only looked as if I was listening.

"When was this?" I managed to butt through the drip of words.

"Four years ago at Las Vegas."

"This is important. Had she any special girl friends?"

"Girl friends!" She checked herself. "Yeah, she had one. Birds of a feather, if you ask me. Called herself Valda and had an act with a couple of tame bears."

I remembered seeing it a few years back. Spectacular, but I could only remember the bears.

"Very thick?"

"As thieves." She slammed her glass down and added a jigger of rum.

"Is Valda around?"

She gave me the pitying look reserved for those who don't read *Billboard*. "She went to Paris two years ago and is doing damned well. That's where I should be."

"Know Valda's real name?"

She thought for a minute and said, "Joan. Joan Jageur. I don't know how she spelt it, but that's how it came out."

I hung around for a while and eased myself out. She nodded to me absently, deep in thought. I gave Cy's palm a gentle press and wished him well.

I went home, peered into the empty cupboard just in

case the first time was a hallucination. It wasn't. I sighed, showered, and carefully selected a suit. It was good old English blue serge, cut business-wise, a little less than sophisticated. I added a Countess Mara tie a good bit too brilliant for the suit. And I took a cab to Marcello's apartment.

Of course, it was in the tower of the building. The liftman was a pimply nineteen-year-old. A sly glance over my shoulder revealed that he was fiddling with the lift gate, pretending not to be watching. I boldly pressed the buzzer on Marcello's door.

I had never caught her act, just paused to leer at the photos outside the places she had worked. She was maybe five feet one. Her face was impudently made, a little mouth, nose slightly snubbed, eyebrows curved in an innocent questioning. She was a glowing natural blonde, with everything that went with it.

I'd got the act worked out in my mind. A hog raiser from Iowa who had taken a trip to Gay Paree and met her friend with the bears. At that, the tongue-tied expression on my face was half natural as I stared down at this delicious morsel.

"I, er, I'm Frank Hodkinson," I blurted, clutching my hat in sweaty paws.

Her voice was a saucy contralto. "I've known many Frank Hodkinsons. All were officers and gentlemen."

I took a backward step, warming up to it.

"I, er, know Joan. I mean Valda. In Paris, France."

"Come in. Any pal of my pal Valda's a friend."

The apartment had been done regardless, I guessed by one of the plushiest consultant firms. It was as though Marcello had instructed them to model a cry, "I'm not a crum. I'm not dirty little Harry Marcello the guy who hangs around poolrooms and does errands for a buck a time. I'm big Marcello. Big! Big!"

The huge living-room had a sunken pool with a little fountain playing. It was divided into two by a glass wall, reaching halfway to the ceiling, in which myriads of tropical fish formed a changing pattern of vivid colour.

I sank into a chair which looked uncomfortable and wasn't.

"A drink?"

I guessed I'd have a little rye, and she came back with a gin for herself. I don't know why, but if the girls who have come up through the chorus like to drink, it's gin.

I told her about Paris, how Valda was the greatest girl I'd known. How she said to be sure and look up her old pal if I came to New York. I blurted out that I'd had to come to the big city on business. I made it unconvincing, as though I'd whipped up my nerve to see her. She was flattered. We had another drink.

She had made a plane trip for ten days to Paris shortly after Valda got there. Fortunately I know Paris well enough to prattle about the sort of places she would have gone to. I had to be careful on names. She could trap me easy. I didn't play it too hard. A few of the people I said I knew. Others I said I did not remember.

One turn of luck came my way. We'd both met up with a middle-aged roué with the title of count. After about six pernods he thinks he has got a mole burrowing away in each armpit and starts taking his clothes off. I dwelt on that and made it funny.

We had three or four more drinks. I watched her carefully. She was wearing jeans and a cashmere sweater, nothing fancy. If I hadn't seen the photos, I wouldn't have thought she had those firm curves. Clothed she looked almost fragile, with no hint of those firm, flat dancer's muscles and the swell of thorax and thigh.

By the time it got round to her switching a standard lamp on, so that the light diffused softly and the tetras in the tank glowed like little points of blue fire, she had perched on the arm of my chair.

It was time for the corny trick. I made an excuse to open my wallet and let Harry's photograph drop out. It fell face downwards and she pounced on it.

"Your wife or girl friend?" She turned it over and I saw recognition on her face.

"My best friend," I said as cornily as I could muster it. "Died recently. Guess I'm sentimental."

The gin was working. Her beautiful face wrinkled. "Funny," she said. "I knew him. His name was Dick, but Marcy said it was Harry. Funny, when I met him his wallet fell open and a man's photograph dropped out."

I roared with laughter. "And I guess you recognised that one too?"

She was laughing with me, the easy gin laughter that can turn as suddenly to tears. "And at that I did. Or I thought I did until I looked close. A friend of Marcy's, only when I looked close it wasn't."

Now was the time to slide, to change the subject.

"Do you know," I said, "I've never caught your act? Tomorrow night, baby, I'll be ringside, bellowing like a bull."

I'd maybe underestimated her capacity. When she slid erect she stood straight, gazing down at me out of her saucy eyes.

"For that, Frank, I'll give you a private audition." She avoided my hands with a neat sidestep and walked to the record-player and put a disc on. "I'll change into my costume. When I yell 'cue' you switch it on."

I guessed it wouldn't take her long to put on the gauze wisps she called a costume. It wasn't long. She called out and I switched the machine on and a long drumbeat faded into a slowish guitar and castanet arrangement.

She came through the door with a lithe rush. I was backing towards the chair. I froze. She hadn't bothered about the costume. Whatever could be said, she was an artist. I perspired. My hand groped and found the whisky. Without moving my head I gulped and felt the drips cold on my chin and throat. The music stopped. I dropped into the chair.

She stood, hands akimbo. "Like it?"

I nodded.

"Repeat?"

I nodded.

"Then *mit*, partner. *Komm mit*!"

In the dim light a middle-aged serge-clad detective postured and pirouetted. She threw herself into my arms. I never realised the muscles you have to have, to catch maybe ninety-eight pounds of delicious-smelling flesh.

"No," she said. "You must be in costume, too."

It took a minute to sink in. Then I heard a shrillish voice saying, "No, baby!"

She stuck her tongue out. "Yes, baby," she said firmly.

Baby was obedient.

The record finished. Somehow I found her perched on my left shoulder.

"Forward march." Her voice was low and thick. I guess she must have ducked as I marched through the room and through the bedroom door.

Sometime in the night, I said drowsily, "You take a chance with Marcy."

"I can handle him," she said, almost maternally.

I bit back the thought that I wondered about me.

"Funny thing, you knowing my friend," I said instead.

"Yeah. It was funny. He said he was a big advertising man from Chicago, he certainly flashed a big roll. Marcy said he was really some cheap newspaper guy out on the tiles." She gave her provocative, aphrodisiac, bell laugh.

"Marcy cross?"

"At first. Then he got the angle and we had a laugh about it, but, hell, honey, must we talk?"

We didn't. The lady's always right.

She was sleeping when I planted a goodbye kiss near her left ear. Opposite the apartment a medium-sized guy pretended to do up his shoelace. His clothes might have cost money: on him everything would look flashy and cheap. I shrugged and hailed a cab. After ten minutes the cabbie said, "A change of form, Mr. Piron." I peered at the identification picture and recognised a driver who had once been a witness in a divorce case I had handled.

"Hallo, Dutch," I said. "How come?"

"You tail people," he said. "You're being tailed. Watch my mirror." He turned left at some lights and stalled his engine. By the time he got started a cab crawled up behind. In it was the flashy guy who'd been fiddling with his shoelaces.

"Want I should lose him? The other driver's a friend of mine. He'll play if I tip him off."

"Hell, no," I said, "don't bother."

It was a bit before eight and the office was deserted except for the nightman on the switchboard, who sat dozing in his chair.

My serge suit was creased and had sticky stains on the jacket. They smelled like gin.

I looked in the cupboard in my room. Usually I keep a spare suit there, the travails of detection being what they are. Unfortunately the current spare was a two-toned job I had bought during a weak-minded moment in Miami. In May in New York it would type me as, maybe, a semi-successful dice player. I did my best to rectify it by taking out the heavy white shirt and black tie I keep around for funerals.

The pint-sized shower-room barely fits my six feet and a hundred and eighty pounds, but I persevered, seeking by nearly scalding water to wash away the grey listlessness that creeps in the wake of debauch.

By the time I had finished, the Old Man was in, hunched over his desk.

"Here," he grunted and tossed over a thin sheet of copy paper.

It had the air of anonymity, even the face of the electric typewriter looked featureless. I read:

S. Drinking Habits. We do not employ drunks or compulsives and use periodic check. Best of our belief S. a moderate drinker.

Bodleigh. Known. One-time employed Government, dismissed grounds of mental instability. Knew S. as a child. Inventor of some promise. Last heard of St. Louis.

Marcello. Known. No convictions since 1946, but history of violence. S. was assigned to contact Marcello's mistress, real name Gwenda Stein, stage name Merlina. Nothing known except fond of men. S. employed the trick of dropping a photograph, retouched so that at a close look Gwenda Stein retracted identification. Subject was a smuggler believed to specialise in bringing high denomination notes and jewellery from behind Curtain. Marcello alleged to change hot money and jewellery on percentage. S. disliked the assignment: Marcello threatened him and we thought it best to relieve him of the case. END.

I scratched my head. I supposed if my wife were as beautiful as Gretyl, I might, with a very small might, ask to be relieved of Merlina. The Old Man watched me as I burned the note with my lighter and stirred the ashes to powder.

I gave him a run-down on what had happened, omitting the more intimate details because I knew the lascivious old monster was dying to hear them.

"So," I concluded, "I can only continue to blunder around, making as much noise en route as possible, hoping it will smoke somebody out."

"Marcello's smart," he said, absently tapping his pipe on the desk. "I've enquired around. He takes care not to be one of those guys the columnists mention, but he's pretty big."

"I've heard a little about the guy," I said. "They say his old man used to peddle fish, which is maybe why he keeps tanks of them in his living-room."

"While you were running around, I called into Headquarters and took a look at Marcello's file."

That was typical. While I scrape favours from desk sergeants, the Old Man is upstairs in the big private office sipping decent Scotch.

"Get this picture," he said. "There was a guy named

Gustave Marcello who had been born in Alexandria, Egypt.
He came to this country in 1911 and kept a small fish shop.
He and his wife both died in 1928. They had a son registered as John Marcello, born 1916. Now it happened
that in 1945 the Department started deporting a lot of the
hoods who didn't have American nationality. They got
quite a few of them. Marcello was on the list. The
Immigration boys poked around and there was precisely no
information around concerning Marcello between the age
of eight, when he was orphaned, and when he was booked
twelve years later for trying to stick up a gas station."

In the silence that followed I could hear my wrist watch
tick.

"They really tried to find out?"

"Yep. I don't have to tell you they are good. There's no
record of a John Christopher Marcello being in any orphan
asylum or attending any school."

I shrugged. The unfortunate thing about cases with maybe
an espionage angle is that you constantly bump into melodramatic possibilities.

"There are plenty of orphanages and adoption societies,
some not legitimate. He could have found a home with
people in another state and used their name for his schooling."

"At that," he said, "it would be a great front. Plant a
young guy with the right indoctrination and tell him to make
himself the reputation of a hood. Nobody would dream that
he's anything else."

"I think, sir, that our Mr. Brown has been something less
than frank. Plainly, the weasel is probably holding back
about ninety-eight per cent."

I thought, "And maybe you are."

There was no reply. He fumbled in his desk. "Better wear
that."

I adjusted the nylon belt and put the gun in the elastic
holster fitting snugly over my kidneys. This set-up is prefer-
able to the shoulder-holster, which is liable to show and is
the first place anybody ever looks. The gun was a custom-
made thirty-eight, so light that you have to get it overhauled

after thirty rounds or so have been fired. You sacrificed accuracy to some extent, but a pistol is only effective at close-range stuff in spite of the films and TV.

I got up to go. He was looking worried.

"Piron," he said, "if you want out, it's okay by me. We'll give the lady a negative report. As for you, the San Francisco office need temporary help for a couple of months."

It was so unlike him that I almost took the offer. I like San Francisco. Stubbornness made me shrug and guess I'd get on with the job. I was to wish I hadn't.

In the front office there is a direct telephone which is listed in the book as belonging to the Grimond Employment Agency. First I got on to the public library and asked the information service what magazines an industrial chemist would read.

Apparently these days there are as many varieties of industrial chemist as there are fish on Fridays. I said I didn't know that, and the young lady expressed well-educated surprise and finally relented by giving me the names of half a dozen magazines she thought would have general appeal to anybody in the industry.

Then, using the Grimond Employment Agency name, I telephoned the magazines, two of which were issued in Detroit. I told them we had a job which would suit Mr. James Bodleigh. We had a St. Louis address, but would they please check their subscription list, and, in the case of the Detroit people, telephone me collect. It was all very urgent. A couple of them wouldn't play, but the other four would.

I sat there and waited for the replies. They all came through in half an hour. Two were negative. The others had Bodleigh on their cards and told me he had changed from St. Louis six months ago and was at a New York address which they gave me.

I got my hat and, after a peek through the window, a raincoat. Outside there was a nip in the air and the clouds were blackish overhead. Before I cased Bodleigh, I decided to have a look at the old dame whom Mrs. Siskin was visiting at the time of her husband's death.

The hotel was still a good one, fighting hard against the chromium and glass palaces. It was quiet, the food was reputed to be good. Once it had been fashionable, but the carriage trade had moved on, leaving it to the older generation and people who considered that at the price it was a good buy.

I knew the house detective, a retired fraud-squad cop named Peabody. He was a dapper little man with a very slight limp. We exchanged pleasantries while he peeped at me warily through his narrow grey eyes. House detectives don't like private richards around.

I put him out of his misery. "It's Mrs. Dymphna Sherrot, who has got a suite here. We got her tabbed as co-respondent in two cases."

He grinned. "Fine old lady. Didn't know she was so active."

Peabody thought that the old lady wouldn't see eighty-five again. She'd moved in twenty-seven years ago and still occupied the same suite. According to the credit agencies she was well loaded. The hotel staff made a pet of her, only partly because she tipped better than average. She had a companion, a trained nurse named Mrs. Wych. That was new to me.

"How's the old lady up top, Tom?" I asked.

He shrugged. "Up to a few years ago she was bright as a button. Almost overnight she changed.. Now she's still pretty active physically for her age, but some days she can't recognise anybody she hasn't known for thirty years. She has good days and bad days. And now, what's it all about, Jim?"

"I guess you were in on the enquiries in January. A homicide dick named Gould would have been round."

He nodded. "A go-getter. Something funny there. There was a suicide verdict, but, the day after, Gould was round, here again. As far as I remember the wife spent most of the day here with another girl, seeing the old lady."

"The point is, could Mrs. Siskin, that's her name, have slipped out for maybe half an hour?"

He shook his head and then shrugged. "I went round the staff. No evidence either way. It's like this, this place is screwed right down to minimum staff. The policy is that they pay rather higher than the other hotels of its class, but they have fewer on the payroll. We don't have waiters and doormen and bus boys hanging round with time to notice things. They're all working like hell."

"Except you, Tom."

"Believe you me, Jim, I bustle around even when I haven't anything to do. The manager's got X-ray eyes, and the dough is a nice addition to a cop's pension."

"Could I see the old lady?"

He peered at his pipe for guidance. "She doesn't sleep much," he said. "Most probably she's in her living-room now. But I'll have to come with you, Jim. She's an old lady, and if I decide so, you get out. Right?"

I nodded.

The door of Mrs. Sherrot's suite was opened by a very thin character, with greying, carroty hair done in some kind of complicated knot. She had no make-up on her leathery face.

She jutted her jaw forward and stared at us.

"Mrs. Wych," said Peabody with professional suavity, "I'd much appreciate it if we could have ten minutes with Mrs. Sherrot. This is Mr. Piron. It's a professional matter. Of course, if she's unwell today . . ."

"Ten minutes," her thin lips snapped at us.

"Here we are, here we are, Mrs. Sherrot, visitors early in the morning," she declaimed in tones which I guessed were meant to be soothing but came out as a harsh, shrill piping with an overlay of aggressive gentility.

Mrs. Sherrot was very small, with apparent frailty. A shawl was wrapped round her shoulders and I noticed the air was chilly.

She caught my glance. "Can't stand central heating, never could. Mrs Wych turns it right down. What's your name, young man? Piron? I knew a Piron once. Nasty fellow, blackballed when he tried to join my husband's club."

"Probably my father," I said.

Her great blue eyes, misted with age, twinkled. "Or great-grandfather is what you're thinking."

This was one of the old girl's good days, I supposed.

I was unpleasantly conscious of Mrs. Wych's eyes boring into my back as I said, "On January 20th, which was a Saturday, your niece by marriage from Chicago spent the day with you here. With her was a Mrs. Siskin: Gretyl. What I want to know is whether Mrs. Siskin could have slipped out for half an hour during that time."

"A policeman, an unpleasant young man, was here about that, Mrs. Sherrot."

I cursed inwardly as the boring voice cut through. The old lady's eyes, which had been alert, suddenly clouded. "A policeman, you say, Mrs. Uh. Extraordinary. I don't remember a policeman."

"His name was Gould," intoned Mrs. Wych.

"I don't know anything about a policeman. The late Commissioner used to come out on Sunday. He and Ralph were friends, you know. Let me see, a nice man but I can't remember his name. I'm afraid I can't help you, Mr. Uh."

I gave her a deep bow and smile and we went out. Mrs. Wych had sure as hell bitched up the deal.

She let us out without a word.

I went back to Peabody's office.

"I'd like to cut a slice of that Wych dame's throat."

"Here, try one of these cigars. Sure, so would a lot of people."

"Any particular reason?"

"You saw her. Mind you, she's completely and utterly devoted to the old lady. Apart from when she's ordered to stay in bed by the doc and they get in a night nurse, the Wych person does all the looking after. The old lady makes her take Sundays off and gets in another woman."

I smoked the cigar. The police report had stated that

while the two women and Mrs. Sherrot were downstairs lunching and gossiping, she remained in her room in the suite except for fifteen minutes when she went down to the coffee room and had a sandwich. She thought the party took about two-and-a-half hours. She'd heard Gretyl enter the suite. Gretyl had called out, "It's me, Mrs. Siskin, Mrs. Sherrot left her wallet on the table."

Mrs. Wych hadn't replied. Gould had asked her how long she estimated Gretyl spent in the suite. Wych had replied, "I don't know, I was engrossed in a book." I could hear her saying it.

Chagrin must have crept onto my jowls. With the old lady in a lucid groove, I could have cleared this particular end up with a little luck.

Peabody tapped my arm. "Piron," he said, "you did me one or two favours when I was on the Squad. I don't forget. If you'll keep me out of it, I've got a small fact."

"I'll keep you out, Tom," I said fervently.

He waggled his cigar to the side of his mouth, looking all cop as he did it. "After Gould had eager-beavered around the first time, I asked the switchboard girls if anybody had phoned out of the Sherrot suite around two thirty—that was the approximate time Mrs. Siskin went for the wallet. The girl said there was a call."

"What number, Tom?" I was agog.

He shook his head. "Hell, we don't track local calls. The girl just blue-ticks the working sheet, one local call to room number so and so."

Less agog, I digested the fact. "If La Siskin made that call, then the Wych dame must have heard it. Unless she's deaf."

"Better hearing than average, to my knowledge, Jim. Anyway, there it is."

I thanked him, half wishing he hadn't told me about the call, which I knew would keep me awake half the night puzzling its place on the board.

"By the way, Tom, I didn't see the phone call mentioned in Gould's report."

He squirmed a little in his battered old swivel chair. "It was like this, Jim, I couldn't see it had the slightest bearing on whether the Siskin woman kept in the hotel or went out and clobbered her old man."

In the cab out to James Bodleigh's place I wished I'd asked him to probe around on the Wych dame. I toyed with the idea that I would stop the cab and phone him. Then I remembered that Tom had a grown-up family who were always dunning him for money : his son couldn't keep a job, the daughter was sickly and spent a lot of her time in hospital. Therefore, Tom needed the money the hotel gave him each week, and if he thought unnecessary peeping on guests would jeopardise it I'd come up against a brick wall. I filed the problem away among the other little ones I carried around.

Bodleigh lived in a fair to middling district, but in one of those brick boxes where the address sounds good until you look inside the little concrete square with its day bed, microscopic bath and toilet, and miniature kitchen.

He was smallish, running to flabby fat, with swimmy eyes behind thick glasses, and a lot of hair which could have done with half an hour at a barber shop. Greasy skin filled in the unprepossessing picture. He was neatly and well dressed in medium-income-bracket clothes.

He blinked at me and told me to come in. The room was clean and the day bed made up. A form sheet and a scratch pad covered with figures were on the little veneered table.

I pulled out a chair, but he preferred to sit on the day bed. His clasped hands writhed and twisted and I saw his nails had been bitten right down.

"I'm enquiring into the death of the late Harry Siskin," I said.

I might have asked the price of milk for the impression it made. "I read he committed suicide," he said indifferently. He had a rather high, slightly flutey voice, not unimpressive, with a pedantic undertone.

"You glad?"

"Should I be?"

I kept my jaw jutted out and a deadpan look, and got up to let him see my height and breadth of shoulder if he hadn't seen them before, and strolled around the little room peering here and there. Then I got straddled back on the chair.

"Bodleigh," I said, "why not co-operate and just answer civil questions? There's a pleasant way to do things."

I let the implication drift awhile.

"Would you like a man who'd robbed you?" His voice was a little shriller. "What should I call you—lieutenant?"

"As we're having a friendly chat, nothing official about it, you might just call me Piron."

I lit a cigarette slowly, not looking directly at him. He cleared his throat.

"I see you figure out the horses, Mr. Bodleigh. Got anything for today?"

"No," he said, "I fancy nothing for today." I let the silence hang in the air and studied the caps of my shoes.

"You know," he said, "you can't bet every day and make money."

"You manage to make money?"

His laugh was short and bitter. "Since you found me here, I can't think how, but no matter, you must know that I'm a chemist, a good one with degrees and documents to prove it. But evidently I am unemployable in the present system."

I made a note of his use of the word "system".

"So you make a living by betting. You must be astute to do that."

He smiled. I thought that the more flattery you fed him the more his appetite for admiration, his capacity for self-pity, would grow, until he became insatiable for heavier dose upon heavier dose. Eventually, it would be impossible to find a heavy enough load to pour into him and he would quarrel, getting his kicks masochistically.

"It's not too hard to do, Mr. Piron, granting certain things. Originally it was a toss-up whether I specialised as a chemist or as a mathematician. I've got a thorough grasp of the laws of distribution. So when the world seemed very black to me I started out to make a thorough study of horseracing. Four hours a night for six months was enough."

"Why don't you sell some of the big gamblers your methods?"

He laughed, a little whicker of mirth. "I would if they'd take a four-year university course first and be prepared to live on what I do."

"Uh, uh," I said.

"You see, I only bet on maybe four races each week, and only certain classes of races. And when I was starting, an insurance policy my parents took out for me at birth matured—three thousand dollars. It must have seemed a lot of money forty-five years ago. With that capital I've averaged sixty dollars per week for nearly two years. If I tried to double that sum I'd be broke within three months."

I wasn't very interested, except that it placed him at the same age as Harry Siskin.

"You were the same age as Siskin? Know him as a kid?"

The bitter edge was back on his tongue. I could almost hear him tasting the words before he expelled them in old venom.

"Oh, yes, dear Harry was always head boy at school. Right out of the good books. I was a puny kid with bad eyesight. There was always God Harry around when the other kids picked on me. Most times. Of course, Piron, it entirely prevented my ever acquiring self-confidence or the other kids accepting me, as they would have in time, but gods never think of that."

"And you met him here after a number of years and he helped you find some money."

"Four hundred dollars." He hissed the words. "If it hadn't been mucked, yes mucked, he'd have had the trivial little return of maybe five million or so. Oh, yes, he'd have taken it in his lordly way."

"If you don't mind, what was it? And remember they didn't do chemistry around my school."

"I don't imagine so. Very broadly, it concerned lubrication. You probably think in terms of mineral oil in crank cases, graphite in pumps. But without annoying the F.B.I. I think I can refer to lubricating the tiny, intricate mechanisms around Government plants. Let's say I originated an amazingly improved method of achieving it."

"And it didn't work?"

"It did, it did, that's the point."

"Oh, I can't see . . ."

"I can see." There was a savage cello note in his voice. "I can see. My device is currently being used. One of the people I approached sold me out."

"You think that it was Siskin?"

"He hadn't the brains to understand the process. He may have organised it, I never thought of that. At school he was a big ox who wanted to write bits for the papers. I've got a case of documents which prove how I was robbed. It's in store, no room here. Come over one night and I'll have it here. I'll give you my telephone number."

I could feel the sick, nervous energy as he bounced over to the table and scribbled. When I took the twist of paper I saw that in spite of his excitement the writing was small, precise, with a couple of ostentatious curlicues to it.

"I surely will, Mr. Bodleigh. Only thing I can't see is why you got mad at Siskin if you weren't sure he instigated the steal."

His voice became calm, slightly exasperated. "He had achieved his little ambition, he scribbled for the papers. When I put it to him that he should expose what had happened in print, he refused. If a man refuses you help to prevent you from being robbed, he's as bad as the thief."

There wasn't an ashtray. Apparently he didn't smoke. I stubbed my cigarette out against the top of my lighter.

"So he was murdered, eh?" There was the feeling of a cat looking at a dying mouse in his voice.

"Now why should you say that?"

"Come now, Piron. The police don't go round probing into suicides a couple of months or so later."

"You're an astute man, Mr. Bodleigh. I wouldn't like all our suspects to have your brains."

"Suspect? I suppose so." He was having an emotional field day and his eyes were glazed in consummation. "I suppose so. Wait a minute."

He reached into the small corner closet and came out with a fat black book. "You learn to be methodical in my profession. What was the date?"

"January 3rd," I said, watching his face.

He flipped through the book quite naturally, "Hm," he said. "I spent the day mostly in bed with a cold. No alibi."

Eager anticipation was in his face.

"Hell," I said, "maybe my brain's getting wet. It was January 20th."

He gave me a long look to show he wasn't fooled and checked again. "This is better. I don't touch the horses the first three months of the year. And I practically don't drink. But I spent the afternoon in Sandy's Bar off Broadway. It's nicely heated and I nursed a couple of Scotches until around six. I hope you don't think it's too sinister that I recollect he was discovered late afternoon."

I remembered Sandy's Bar, a place where the seedier horse players congregated and talked shop so regularly that the rumour was that the sandwiches were lined with hay.

"Sandy's Bar? Queer place for you."

"It amuses me to hear them talking in thousands when they haven't got the price of a decent apartment. They think I'm a queer bird, Piron. I just sit and listen and laugh inside. None of them has a child's inkling of the laws of probability."

I scratched the side of my chin. Most of the inhabitants of Sandy's Bar did their sleeping at places like Pablo's Palace.

"You seem in the clear, Mr. Bodleigh. Trouble is that those guys have memories that make a sieve look solid, unless it's racing form."

He looked superior. "They may remember by association. There was a big heavyweight fight that night. Joe, that's the barman, asked me my opinion. I know nothing of such matters, but I said I thought the younger, fitter man would win, as of course he did."

I got up and went to the door. He shook my hand and his palm was greasy with sweat.

"You'll phone?"

"Surely."

His eyes narrowed. "If I were you I'd take a close look at Siskin's wife." Lust mixed with hate in his expression.

"Anything concrete?"

"I know women like that." He shut the door dramatically. I called into the nearest bar and took a double Scotch to wipe the taste away. All this had taken longer than I thought. It was twelve, so I took a cab to the newspaper office where Siskin had done casual work. I got in to see the Features Editor. He was a rangy man named Groom with the longest pointed nose I had ever seen on a man and a pair of piercing blue eyes set close to its bridge. He chain-smoked and talked quickly. He was the guy to whom Siskin had made the remark about resigning from homo sapiens.

He'd seen Siskin a couple of times the week he died, as well as the Friday and Saturday morning he was working.

"I gather Harry sometimes turned down work here when it offered?"

"Sure. He was a strange guy. We all are. I'd had to tell him that if he kept on knocking back week-end work the office manager would strike him off the roster. He took it all right. He was a big amiable guy usually."

Siskin worked on the Sunday supplement, cutting articles, writing heads and leads, working up fillers when there was a hole in the page. "He was a good desk man," said Groom, "and only a run-of-the-mill reporter. If he'd held a regular job he'd have probably made good on the executive side— he was one of those fellows that you can't help liking, ideal for a manager."

"Was he soft?"

"Hell, no, you never got the idea you could push Siskin around. Somehow the situation never arose with him."

That last week there had been something wrong with Siskin. He appeared tense and even surly, almost lost his temper at some office joke or other, Groom couldn't remember what.

I went to see the other man whose name appeared on the police file. It turned out he was the office manager, a squat, chesty man named Bertaux, with snapping eyes and a personality to match his build that hit you when you faced him over the desk. Unlike Groom, he was calm and relaxed.

"Why the post-mortem interest in poor Harry, Piron?"

"The widow isn't satisfied with the police report."

"Is there a story?"

"I doubt it. I don't think there's any secrecy, if you wanted to run a par, perhaps good publicity for us."

He made a note on a pad. "I shouldn't think there's anything in it for us, but I'll tell the city editor. I checked with you first because I liked Harry and dog doesn't eat dog, if you follow me."

"I understand you threatened to bounce him if he refused offers of work."

His black eyes were expressionless as. he said: "I can't play favourites behind this desk. We keep a roster and every man on it gets a fair crack of the whip. That way we're insulated against people going sick when we put the supplement away. I had a word with Groom, to make it informal, and he tipped off Harry."

"Any resentment?"

"With Harry? Hell, no! He had a drink with me and said he was sorry he'd put me on the spot."

"I want you to think carefully. Could he have been a hotel-room drinker?"

There is one thing about most newspapermen, you don't have to underline the score.

Without hesitation he shook his head. "I've been out with Harry quite a few nights when his wife, Gretyl, was out of town. A couple of times we were tearing around. Siskin could take it or leave it, believe me, brother. I see plenty of lushes around this job, but Harry wasn't one."

He agreed that the last week had seen Harry with something on his mind. In his words Siskin had the black dog on his shoulder and didn't seem able to throw it off.

"You know his wife?"

"Gretyl. Sure. We worked together on a Denver paper after her first husband died."

"What's she like?"

He shrugged. "I'm a guy that thinks women have no business around the industry. Back in Denver I was assistant to the city editor, the guy who took all the kicks."

"And she was a kicker?"

"Not in the way you mean. You see, Piron, once in a while a newspaper starts an exposé campaign. Say the local hospital is serving third-grade meat. Okay you run it, but the art of editing is to close off before the public get tired. If you don't, circulation slips and the floor is covered with severed heads. No good. But take Gretyl, she couldn't understand why her latest campaign—cruelty to cats or what-have-you—could not go on until every cat had a bed of its own and caviar for breakfast. And I was on the receiving end."

"Good at her work?"

"Fair descriptive stuff. I used to tell her she should get a job writing colour leads for an agency."

"Man-hungry?"

He shrugged. "She's a good person and when I knew her she was recovering from the drunken brute she'd married. Matter of fact, my wife introduced her to Siskin. He was down on some kind of story and had an introduction to me. He returned the favour later by tipping me that the job here was going to be open."

His telephone rang. I said I wouldn't take up any more of his time and walked through the faint smell of hot metal you always get in newspaper palaces to the lift.

Outside a niggling drizzle had begun, unpleasantly whipped by a faint breeze, and I went into a restaurant and had minestrone and a slice of pizza. Afterwards every taxi seemed hired so I caught a bus, crowded with fairly wet and irritable people. It took me the best part of an hour to get to the Siskin apartment. It was one of a block of four with a fairly pleasant prospect around it. A smallish woman with a round face and glasses opened the door. She wore street clothes and seemed flustered.

"Mrs. Siskin in? Name's Piron."

She hesitated and scuttled away. I followed, down a passage and into the living-room. I presumed it was the living-room. Lying on a rug was Gretyl Siskin and my gaze riveted on three feet of leg. Through the daze my brain registered that she was dressed in maybe enough fabric to cover my two hands. Her head was propped on a fancy rubber pillow. The other woman was staring at me, with her eyes attempting to pop through her glasses. I registered her as a nice homely type, well dressed.

The burnished head turned on the pillow and the green eyes fixed on mine.

"Oh," she scrambled up with a lithe flashing of white, slightly tanned legs and went through the door, leaving behind her the smell of perfumed woman.

The little old lady shifted from one leg to another in embarrassment. She tried to speak and a squeak emerged. My face told me the central heating was turned full up, but something else made my skin prickle. I had thought that my encounter with Merlina had stilled those carnal lusts considerably, but, no, Old Adam was stirring.

She was back almost immediately, in long-legged strides, wearing a housecoat. The stain of a flush was on her neck and cheeks.

"It's all right, Aunt," she said. "This is Mr. Piron, the nice detective. No need for you to stay."

"Are you sure you'll be all right?" the old lady half-whispered.

Gretyl laughed and the dimple showed. "Oh, sure, run along. I'll call in this evening."

We heard the front door close. I looked out the window.

Irrationally I was glad my raincoat hid the flashy suit I was wearing.

"Won't you take your coat off?"

"No," I said, "I won't be long."

She gestured to the floor. I saw that the rug was littered with bright travel pamphlets: exotic palm-covered islands looking larger than life; gay cafés with striped awnings and romantic waiters where you pay a dollar twenty-five for a cup of coffee; flagstoned courtyards with copper urns, and the flies not showing in the four-colour printing.

"Vicarious pleasures?"

She nodded. "I'm glad you don't think I'm mad. After Harry died I thought of taking a trip. Then I decided it was simply escapism, but when I'm low I get out these brochures and just dream I am lolling on some sunlit beach thousands of miles away."

"Logical," I said. Through the window I could see it was grey and misty and the rain was starting to come down real hard.

"Would you like a drink?" She was wearing one of those wraps you can never get to close really tight. My lips felt dry.

"Sure, make it something exotic to go with the scenery."

She looked at me sharply, but I was apparently peering at a double-spread of Venice.

Presently she came back with two glasses. I tasted and found a variation on daiquiri cocktail. It was good. I found a chair and sat.

"Okay, Mrs. Siskin, you'll want a progress report. I've seen the Pablo Hotel and it's plain that people could get in and out with a good chance of not being noticed at that hour. I don't think Marcello remained steamed up at your husband, just a passing gust as it were."

"You saw that gangster?"

I shook my head. "He's in Las Vegas—I hope. I saw his lady."

For the first time her eyes really appraised me as a man. She couldn't help asking, "What's she like?"

"The kind of woman who so worried the Crusaders when they went off for a year or two. By the way, your husband's interest was purely professional. He saw her a couple of times and tried to pump her about a particular branch of Marcello's business—changing hot money."

"Oh." It could have meant anything.

"Okay. Next, John Bodleigh is in town. He didn't care for your husband and doesn't like you."

"He made me sick. His eyes . . ."

"Sure. I wouldn't put him as a killer, except that if Harry was killed, the method obviously was an ingenious one, and Bodleigh's a real cutie from way back. Lastly, there's no doubt that your husband had something on his mind that last week. What I have to establish is a likely method whereby somebody lured your husband to the hotel and left a bottle of peach brandy where he was likely to try a small snort."

Her eyes narrowed. "He was interested in old New York, as I told you. I did mention to him that maybe a series on the semi-slums, showing what they had been once, might sell."

If she was guilty, she was throwing every lead to me.

"You had peach brandy in the house?"

"Yes," she said, "come and look."

In another room, larger than the one we had come from, was a small built-in bar. There was a good array of bottles. As she had stated, the fancier ones were mostly three-quarters full and included peach brandy, although not the same brand as the bottle containing the cyanide.

We went back and she watched me as I smoked and tried to think.

"Mr. Piron, I wasn't entirely frank with the police." She leaned forward in her chair so that the housecoat slipped away from her lap. I forced myself to watch her face.

I watched her as she walked to the big writing-desk in the corner of the room. From the drawer she produced a small notebook and gave it to me. It was a cheap affair, with the name of a supermarket printed on the cover. Inside, the pages had been ruled off into days of the week, with the store's specials printed in. There were twenty-seven pages and the dates covered December of last year.

Slightly angular writing covered fourteen of the pages. It looked gibberish.

"Your husband's writing?"

"Yes, some kind of a code. I don't know whether you have come across it, but foreign correspondents have a kind of very abbreviated form of sending cables. It's almost pig-Latin. I learned about it when I took journalism at college. This isn't it, but it's something on the same lines."

"Where did you find this?"

She sighed.

"At the time my first reaction was to get out of this apartment and get rid of anything that was Harry's."

Her forearms were flat against her thighs and she seemed smaller and kind of shrunken. I wondered why the urge to destroy the personal possessions of the dead still persisted in modern times: after all, nobody hesitates to take their money.

She straightened up. "I decided I was being irrational and didn't do it. But meantime I had started to pack his books. This dropped out of one of them, an anthology of modern verse he often used."

I slipped the book in my pocket. "I'll have an expert look at it. Did your husband know Latin?"

"It was one of the subjects he majored in."

"If it can be cracked it could be useful."

She said she thought all codes could be cracked and I told her some couldn't, the entirely arbitrary ones where ordinary words have an entirely different, pre-arranged significance.

The rain was sheeting against the window panes and the warmth of the room made me clammily hot with my raincoat on. It was one of those moments when you hear your own voice and that of the person to whom you are talking echoing vacantly in the air. Our voices died away and the silence was heavy.

I said, "Had you or your husband a private income, Mrs. Siskin?"

There was no reason for the flush which greeted the question. She hesitated just too long before she shook her head.

"If you go to a doctor, Mrs. Siskin, you're frank with him. The same with a lawyer. You're paying me your good money. If you can't level, you'd better go elsewhere."

I got up and strolled over to the window. She sat and thought for fully two minutes. Then she asked me what I meant.

"You're not an idiot, Mrs. Siskin, and you worked around newspapers. You must have realised that your husband's way of life couldn't be supported by his freelance activities plus irregular week-end stints. And you were far less than sincere when you threw a remark that he'd paid the premiums on a big insurance policy by stinting on his meals."

I swung round suddenly. Her red lips were parted and I could see her pink tongue licking the lower one. She was breathing quickly.

"Can you give me a cigarette, please?"

She smoked with the nervous puffs of the very occasional smoker. I finished my drink and picked up my hat.

"Don't go." Her voice was low and little-girlish. I put my hands on my hips and stared at her.

"I'm sorry," she said.

"The hell you are." I glared down at her.

"Please sit down, Mr. Piron. I should have told you, but somehow, in your office, it didn't come out. Yes, Harry had another source of income. That's why he could turn down a steady job and live the life he liked."

"Don't tell me he worked magazine subscriptions or printed visiting cards at home." My tone was savage. She annoyed me. Sex antagonism, I guessed.

"Do you have to play tough, Piron?" There was laughter in the green eyes, and hardness too.

"It gets a habit." I sat down.

Her voice became businesslike. "For ten years Harry had worked for a syndicate that bought up old property, tore it down, and erected apartment houses and shopping centres."

"Which one?"

She made a little pushing gesture with both hands. "Let me tell it my own way. Harry knew a great deal about New York. He was an expert, and he knew enough Spanish, Italian and Yiddish to be able to have a lot of friends whom the typical New Yorker would never get to. He had a roving assignment to spot likely city blocks. He found out if the small owners were thinking of selling, what rents were paid, things like that."

I watched her stub out her cigarette with a nervous gesture. Experience told me that she was trying to convince herself that the story she was telling would convince me.

"Harry never told me the name of the people he worked for. The whole essence of the thing was secrecy. If people had known he was the advance agent for big developers, the deals would never have gone through."

By the time she had finished she was sweating. I considered. In a way, it was plausible. The real-estate business is a jungle at the best of times, and there are plenty of undercover men used as scouts, a lot of them part-time, just as there are plenty of guys who earn a dollar looking around for income-tax evasion cases.

"You never asked him the name of these people, Mrs. Siskin?"

"You must believe me. He told me that he would tell me, but it was I who told him that it would be better if I didn't know. I believe, Mr. Piron, in not meddling with my husband's business, even to the extent of not giving advice."

I kept silent on the subject and merely asked if I could go through Siskin's papers. She opened the writing-desk. He'd been a methodical man. In the top were files of receipts, hire-purchase documents, and a ledger listing the dates when he sent out his special articles, when they were accepted, and details of payment. I went through them methodically. It was more or less the picture of Mr. America. A car paid off three months before his death. Harry had been shopping around for a good trade-in deal. The deep freeze had nine months to go, but there had been a two-thousand credit in the bank. Judging by a wad of brochures, he had been considering a small house farther out of town in place of the apartment.

In the cupboard part of the desk were neat carbons of his articles, and a file of personal letters. I read through them. There was nothing significant. I got the impression of a level-headed man who could express himself clearly, but with a hint of pedantry.

I got up and stretched after three-quarters of an hour. While I had been working Gretyl had changed. She wore a rather severely cut grey number and expert make-up. I was glad to see that she knew how to dress.

"Anybody go through those papers, Mrs. Siskin?"

"Only the lawyer I hired to deal with probate. Oh, a few days after Harry was cremated somebody came over from the paper he worked on. They thought he'd taken something home to work on, but they didn't find it, I guess."

I nodded and refused her offer of another drink.

"Mrs. Siskin," I said, "I still don't think you are being completely frank."

She met my stare without flinching. "I've told you what I can."

I fished out a card bearing my private address and telephone number, and laid it on the coffee table.

"You can reach me there out of office hours." I nodded and left her there, tall, beautiful, and, I thought, false.

I made a routine call through to the office manager of Siskin's newspaper.

"Did you send a guy out to look through Siskin's effects?"

"Hell, no! Hang on, I'll make a check."

After five minutes he told me that nobody knew anything about it.

"What gives, Piron? You're getting me very curious."

"Just routine."

It was six thirty when I got back to the office and the Old Man was still there, which was unusual, but it saved me a trip out to his gloomy house. He looked old and tired and dispirited.

"Hell," I said, "I've got a pretty good idea of the trial balance. You should be grinning and handing out bonuses."

"That'll be the day, Piron! How did it go?"

I gave him the report. "And for what it's worth, the Siskin woman knows a hell of a lot more than she gives out."

I let that sink in and then gave a swing to the jaw. "And our little friend, Mr. Brown, is using me as a cat's paw and I don't like it. He sent a guy, pretending to be from the newspaper, to rummage around Siskin's desk. When he does something like that, I want to be told. And I want to see him or the other guy who was Siskin's contact. Or you can put another man on the case."

He looked at me with narrowed eyes. Finally he nodded. "It's fair enough, Piron. I told you that you could go off the case. If you do, I'll just turn it in. But I'll drop a note to Brown, special messenger, and tell him you want a conference."

I left it at that and went home. There was a steak in the deep freeze and I found myself messing around with tomato, canned mushroom and tarragon. I opened a bottle of Californian red wine with an earthy taste about it. The steak was good, but I ate without relish. It was one of those nights when you catch yourself wishing the phone would ring. I switched on the television and switched off at the first commercial. I changed my suit and wandered out. A bachelor gay among all the other bachelors gay who wander the sidewalks because they can't put up with themselves in an apartment.

Dropping into a few clubs, I sought to clutch out and find replenishment for my spirit. I got a smart red-head who bought underwear for a mid-west group of stores. I prattled and prated, very much man-about-town. In the end her flat voice and habit of saying, "So I said to him, look mister," got on my nerves. I bowed out smiling. She may have been disappointed.

The watch hands crawled to quarter to midnight and I found myself in Dick's place not far from the village. A den for serious drinkers, men and women, and a noteworthy quality about the booze. If you want a break from drink you can get the best mixed grill in town. The pub-crawl was going down on expenses, so to be reasonable about it I slipped Siskin's photograph out of my wallet and beckoned to Dick.

"This bird one of your clients, Dick?"

His fat, hairy hand took the print and I saw recognition in his eyes. Dick is one of those guys who can equate faces, names and drinks effortlessly.

"What's it about, Piron?"

"Maybe divorce."

He massaged one of his chins. "I recognise the guy. Pretty sure of it. He came in maybe twice a week, round about six, and had a couple of drinks with a woman."

"When was this?"

"Hell," he said, "time's another thing. I think he started round about ten months ago and, come to think of it, I haven't sighted either of them for some time, as far as I remember."

"Nice dame?"

"If you like 'em maybe fifty-two. Well preserved. A bitter-looking dame who drank London gin. I guess that'd be the wife, maybe."

"The girl friend."

"No accounting for tastes," he said philosophically and waddled away.

After a quarter of an hour I decided against the mixed grill and went on my way. Dick's Bar is at the end of an alley, well lit, so I spotted the three men a second before they rushed me. The blackjack stung my cheek as I threw myself backwards and rolled. A foot kicked my thigh as I jerked the thirty-eight from its resting place in the small of my back and fired onto the paving stones. They weren't gunboys and shied back. I heard the ricochet and one of them gave the convulsive twitch that everybody gives when a bullet hits them.

The leader was a vast, disorganised hulk of a man with a face pounded into vacancy. One of the other two was small, broad and piglike. The other was a thin, sallow youth with pimples.

For a split second we faced each other. Then someone muttered "Scram", and they rushed for the entrance to the alley. There, wearing his usual lop-sided, grimacing smile, was Gould, the Homicide man. His gun looked big in his hand. Blood started to ooze on to the sallow youth's yellow shoe.

I got up and frisked them for him. Apart from the leather-covered clubs they were clean. Presently the wagon came along and we watched them loaded in.

"No hurry," said Gould, "they'll be booked on sus. Better call down at the precinct house tomorrow and sign a complaint. And you owe me a drink."

I thought I'd been doing pretty well on my own, but I took him back to Dick's. He ordered calvados, a pretty fancy drink for a cop.

"Do you have to tag along after me, fellow?"

He leered. "An understanding wife, an understanding lieutenant."

He drained his glass. "I needed that. Do you know, Piron, you've been into seven drinking dens tonight showing your photograph of Siskin?"

"I make it eight."

He shook his head. "Seven, it's down in the little book. Those three guys tagged along to the last three. They were a little late. They work for a guy named Breen. He runs pool halls. Guess who owns Breen?"

I shook my head and fingered the bruise on my thigh.

"Marcello. That reminds me." He crooked his finger. Dick had been urgently at work at the other end of the bar. He caught Gould's eye reluctantly and waddled towards us.

"Dick," said Gould, "who asked you whether Piron was in here?"

The heavy eyes became opaque. "I don't know what you're talking about."

"I think you do," said Gould, without apparent emotion.

His right hand snaked down so that it caught Dick's arm just above the wrist. I hadn't realised the whipcord under the thinness. He pressed down. Dick dropped his shoulder. The cop's hand shifted up and pressed some more. He looked at Dick with the cold, clinical look of a surgeon.

"Dick," he said evenly, "I'll get it, you know—"

Sweat poured down into Dick's pouched eyes. Sullenly he said, "It was Big Tommy Breen. Hell, he must have phoned maybe thirty joints where Piron goes. And Piron can take care of himself. I figure it's maybe a roughing-up. I got to stay in business."

I felt sorry for Dick. He had to stay in business. His life was a constant wrestle against truth. He had to figure which pimp he'd have to bar, exactly how much credit to give a lush, just when you bounce the guy who peddles a little marijuana on the side. Life became a constant ethical game. And the cops. And maybe somewhere there was a Mrs. Dick and a few kids going to good schools.

Gould increased the pressure. "And Big Tom works for who . . . ?"

"For Chris' sake, you're breaking my arm." The tableau was unnoticed. Dick still forced his genial mask to stick. "Okay. The rumble is he works for Marcello."

Gould lifted his arm away. "There you are, son," he said. "It's easy when you try." The fat man was shaking as he moved away.

"Did you have to do that?"

He shrugged and gave me his thin, humourless grin. "I was on the narcotics squad two years, the vice squad three. I worked these places. Take Dick, he makes his money running a joint, a good joint as they go. So he takes the rough with the smooth. He's not forced to."

He looked at me and sipped his drink. "You got the light

squad tonight, Piron. Maybe the men will move in. Marcello knows a few."

I shrugged. "I've met people like Marcello before. I'm still around."

"Piron," he said, "I don't dislike you. A lot of cops don't go for the private boys. Me, I co-operate. I don't think you know too much about Marcello?"

"I don't," I said. "He's one that doesn't advertise."

"Remember the fight last August where a young welter got killed in the ring?"

I nodded. It was one "sport" I didn't like. I'll stomach the bulls, but I don't like to see punk kids smashing each other for an audience of slobs.

"I've even forgotten his ring name. His real was Henry Scarlatti. He was twenty-two, ambitious, and coming up fast. Marcello's building up a sham fight against the champion and the guy he's got as the stooge was fighting Scarlatti. The kid's manager tells him to tank it—take a dive around the seventh and be careful not to cut the stooge, who bleeds like a pig. The kid says no, he can take this punk in three rounds. Maybe so, and the manager runs to Marcello. As Scarlatti is going to the fight, three guys rough him over with blackjacks, plenty of knocks around the head and a good kick in the belly. Not enough to show. Result is that he has brain haemorrhage in the third."

"Nice guy, Marcello."

He nodded. "Quite a few cripples around who once stood upright and crossed him."

"So he's a dirty punk."

"Dick!" He raised a finger. "Another calvados, pally, please, on Mr. Piron." He looked at me. "Piron, I'm going to be an Inspector the day I retire." His voice was a hard monotone. "I'm ambitious and I'm a good cop. Marcello's getting too big. If he keeps on he'll be what Capone was to Chicago. He's got the same mixture of slime, cunning, cowardice and occasional guts that spell danger to me. I want him out."

"Okay by me," I said.

He did his disconcerting quick change. "So I'm going to have an Inspector's funeral with the mayor beside the grave. Therefore when I see a guy living at the rate of twelve thousand a year when he maybe earns nine, I wonder."

I turned in time to get the humourless smile. "Sure," he said, "Siskin. Think I'm dumb? You know, Piron, whenever I see a guy I can tell his income after a time. If there's a gap, maybe I ask did Auntie Nell leave him her Con. Edison stock? If not, he's in my book."

I shrugged. "Maybe Mrs. Siskin had the dough."

He chuckled with no mirth. "Piron, I know what you earn, pretty well. You don't gamble, the dames practically buy their own fodder, and you don't touch stocks, except maybe Mutual Funds. You maybe put away eight hundred dollars each year. Right?"

There'd been a couple of nice bonus years for Piron. Those aside, he was too close for my liking. If it's anything I hate, it's people nosing my finances.

"You're a clever bastard, Gould. You should be an income-tax inspector."

He fiddled with his drink and shot it at me. "Blackmail or dope?"

"What? Me?"

His stiffened finger painfully prodded my breast bone. "Siskin, punk! Sure, I'm going to be an Inspector, but I don't throw dirt about, unless I have to, so I didn't mention it in the report."

"Maybe you'll become Commissioner at that rate. And keep those honest hands away from me, son."

His grin was beginning to annoy me. "I smell around, get a couple of stoolies. Nobody'd heard of Siskin putting on the black or wholesaling heroin."

I shrugged and slipped off the stool.

"Nice to see you, Gould. I'll be at the Inspector's funeral."

He kept his grin. "And mind the broad back, son."

I checked the apartment, threw the mortice lock and checked the bolt and chain, and slept like a log. For four hours: at six o'clock the doorbell rang. I peered out through the peep hole. The face I saw was blond and nordic, pink-cheeked, immaculately shaven, good humoured.

I opened the door, standing behind it, with the thirty-eight ready for action.

He came in in two almost military steps, stopped and extended a piece of paper held in two palmed hands. "And don't shoot the pianist," he said.

I felt slightly foolish as I extended my free hand and briefly glanced at it. "The bearer is okay," the Boss had written, and signed it with his inimitable sign manual.

I am a hospitable type. I have entertained drunks, bores and out-of-town salesmen when I didn't feel like it. I fluttered around in pyjamas like a dowager in Cannes.

"Breakfast? Bacon and eggs?"

"Sure," he said, "but just show me the kitchen and I'll fix. Sorry about this, but Mr. Brown craves action at all times. Go and shower if you like."

I took him at his word and took a tub. As I splashed I tried to place him: his face was tantalisingly familiar.

He was a good cook. The diced bacon and small bread cubes had been fried until they were crisp and incorporated in the eggs, done sunnyside up. More surprisingly, he didn't talk. If he'd been a woman I'd have proposed. As it was, I sneaked glances at his hundred and eighty well preserved pounds. He was about my height, exuding well-being. I placed him as maybe fifty. He had the look of a man twelve years younger.

Finally we came to the coffee and relaxed. His eyes were a disconcerting ice-blue.

"My name's Pout if that means anything."

It clicked. J. R. P. Pout. The family went way back, the kind of family that never got in the gossip columns except when an ex-king of somewhere decided to take a look at a republic. Quiet wealth, family pretty well died out. As I remembered the Pouts had dwindled to three maiden ladies with establishments in Connecticut and J.R.P. The male Pout had been one of the youngest promoted colonels, substantive, after Harvard Business School and a career as a track runner over 1,500 metres. A very good yachtsman, in the running for international event crews, and a mountaineer.

I nodded. "Surprise, Pout. Is your Mr. Brown a Rockefeller?"

He grinned. "Merely a bastard."

He had done something to the coffee. Maybe eggshells. It was very good and I said so.

"We bachelors make good cooks, Piron. I've got a compulsion to be good." He took the cigarette I offered and inhaled deeply.

"I didn't expect you to become one of Mr. Brown's boys."

He laughed, wryly. "If we're going to work together, you might as well know something about me. I've looked at your file and it's extremely impressive. I got into this thing through military intelligence, first in the Italian campaign then in Korea. I hated intelligence work, but when the guns stopped I felt bored. So when Brown got in touch with me, I didn't hesitate. The alternatives were an idle life, the family business, or Brown. So I spent a few years stooging round Europe."

I munched the remainder of my buttered toast. "As you probably know," he said, "it's not all that damned melodramatic, but the constant change of scene suited me. Then, as always happens, the opposing team got on to me."

"Show us your scars," I said.

"The only time I was ever in danger, as far as I know, was in Berlin. One of the night porters was visiting a tourist in her room. He was creeping back along the corridor when he saw a guy fiddling with the lock on my door. Maybe the lady hadn't been kind, but anyway he had the energy to clobber the guy well and good.

"When he'd gone for the police, I went through the fellow's pockets. He'd come prepared to kill me." He shrugged. "Nobody wanted trouble, so he got six months for being on private property with a skeleton key. But it finished me for that type of work. Brown called me back and made me personal assistant here."

I said it always astonished me how all foreign agents in Europe got taped eventually.

He shrugged. "It's just systematic checking. If Mr. X is seen around long enough in certain places he goes on the check list. It might take a week or five years. I was lucky. It took them a bit over eight years."

"Where did you meet Siskin? I take it he never went to your office."

"He didn't even know where it is. He telephoned me every day. If I wanted to see him, I picked him up in a car at an appointed place. I'd drive long enough to check we weren't followed and park. It's the safest method."

"So you never met him at the Hotel Pablo?"

"Hell, no. A hotel room is the last card in the pack. Sometimes we have to use one, but I'd always seen Harry in a car. I'll put you in the picture to the extent that I'd dealt with him for three years. The guy before me retired."

"Okay. Pout, as I worked it out, your Spymaster thought Siskin was getting close and arranged his suicide. In that act he stepped out of his own world and might have bungled. If that's so and he knows I'm prying around, he might try to tie up the loose strings, say by killing Gretyl Siskin. Then you get him."

"That's what Brown thinks." His manicured hands selected a cigarette. He held it with an odd cupping motion.

"And you don't."

He smoked in silence for a few seconds. "I can't add much to what Brown told you. Frankly, I think your security record entitles you to more. But Brown says no and that fixes that. There is a man in this city who organises spying on behalf of China. That's definite. The object appears to be to get a picture of Uncle's military dispositions and the current State Department theory, so the Reds know exactly how tough they can be at any given time. Marcello might be involved, maybe as the money changer. I doubt it. Now, let's take a look at Harry Siskin. Usually the guys I deal with are faces : there's no personal area to our dealing. I keep an eye on them to see they're not turning into alcoholics or anything of that sort, but otherwise I don't know anything about them outside the files.

"Siskin was different. I'd known him for two periods during the war. We'd spent a couple of hot week-ends together in Cairo. That sort of stuff."

He stubbed his cigarette neatly in the ashtray. Personal habits tell you a lot about a man. He seemed hesitant as to how to proceed.

"I'd turned in a report recommending that Siskin should be taken off the job, and either be an inside man in our own or a similar agency, or else be paid off."

"Losing his nerve?"

"His job was not highly dangerous, Piron. No, Harry was getting independent. There is one cardinal rule we have and that is that you do exactly what you're told, no less and no more. If you have to make a choice you always do less. There were two occasions when Siskin went beyond his instructions. After the second I put in my report."

I refilled the coffee cups, and thought of Siskin's photograph and the stubborn set of the jawline. Probably a man very difficult to shift from an idea, great tenacity under a mild, pleasant manner.

Suddenly he said, "What's his wife like? Oh, I've seen photographs. But what about her personality?"

"Likes her own way," I said, "maybe not too scrupulous about how she gets it. An end-justifies-the-means type. Masses of sex appeal, but no nonsense. A queer mixture and far from being as unsubtle as she seems."

He grunted. "The marriage was breaking up. I often told myself that I should put Siskin on to Brown's other assistant. Personal relationships are unhealthy in this job. But Harry was a charmer all right and I liked him very much and, oh, hell!"

"Mrs. S. sounds pretty cut up about his death."

"She's a campaigner, Piron, and never gives up. All sorts of good causes ridden implacably until she drives everybody to distraction. Harry's death has become a Cause to her. Maybe. I guess you've thought that her song-and-dance to you might be a clever front for a murderess?"

His eyes were steel hard. I thought that I would prefer never to come up against him.

I nodded. "It's been known."

"I'm sure there was another woman in Siskin's life. It didn't matter to me because his loyalty was beyond any thought of reproach. It was the case of two strong-willed people. I knew Harry well enough to know that what he liked was fluffy little women who hung on every word. She was as strong as him, that was the trouble."

"What I hoped for," I said, "was a list of the things Siskin had been covering for the last month. I suppose that's out."

"It's out. And, Piron, your file has the word *independent* underlined in red. If you have a lead on Siskin, we want it before you take any action. I'd rather you and I didn't clash."

He stood up and gave me a brief stare before his features lapsed back into pink, pleasant composure.

"Piron good nigger, clean, obedient," I said.

He grinned. "Hell, what a life, eh? Any time you want to see me, I'm in the phone book. If I'm out, the houseman will take a message. And, by the way, Brown doesn't want police activity."

He left behind a faint smell of toilet water. Mechanically I put the dirty plates in the sink. Outside it had started to drizzle again and what sky I could see was dirty and leaden. I massaged the slight ridge of fat that had started to become noticeable around my middle and started to touch my toes fifty times, well knowing that the advancing years were sneering at me and I should probably never find time again.

At the thirty-eighth the doorbell sounded again. I was breathing fast as I got the gun and peeped. This time it was Gretyl Siskin. She had a yellow handkerchief round her head and a thin white raincoat accentuated her curves. I watched the drops of moisture on her face for a few seconds before going back to put the gun away.

She hesitated before she came in. "Mr. Piron. Are you . . . I mean . . ."

"Utmost chastity prevails this morning, Mrs. Siskin."

She looked around the big living-room. "I'm afraid I took it for granted you were a bachelor, Mr. Piron. I don't know why. This is a man's room though."

I waved her to my best chair and she took off the raincoat. Some women can take clothes off gracefully, some can't. She could.

"Mrs. Siskin," I said, "the longer you put off telling me, the harder it will become. So let us cut the social graces."

Partly to make it easy for her, I closed my eyes, and just listened to her husky voice with its strong feminine undertones.

"I didn't lie. I just concealed. First about Harry's other job—the real-estate job. It worried me. I was speaking the truth when I said I told him I wasn't curious. But it was like a fester. Reason told me his explanation wasn't true. He was an antiquarian, a researcher, but he wasn't a real-estate man like any I've ever met, you know what I mean."

"Sure," I said, "so instead of facing him with it you let it fester."

"It didn't show," she said. "I made sure. But every time the telephone rang, I thought, 'This is it, this is where everything falls to pieces.' And then maybe I'd look at Harry and see his solidity and know instinctively he wouldn't do anything crooked."

Opening my eyes I looked at her. Her face was placid and confiding. A hell of a woman, I thought.

"Gretyl," I said, the Christian name coming automatically, "I can tell you one thing very definitely. Your husband was not paid for doing anything even remotely illegal or shady. Period."

"You're not just telling me this?" The words came in a rush.

"Now, look, I'm not going to dwell on this, and what

little I tell you is not for you to repeat. Harry had another source of income, Mrs. Siskin, a confidential one. A woman with your brains shouldn't want anything further."

"You can call me Gretyl if you want," she said, absently. "Oh, I see. I should have thought of it."

"The point is," I said, "that you shouldn't have."

I went and reheated the remainder of the coffee. Her hand trembled a little as she took the cup.

"This is good," she said. "Why is it that men, when they feel like it, cook better than women? Unfair."

"Usually. the repertoire is limited, Gretyl. I eat two kinds of steak, three kinds of stew, when I'm on my own."

"Which wouldn't be often?" Her eyes were shrewd.

"More than I care about." She was talking to get over a sense of shock.

"Coming back to business. What were your relations with Harry? I mean quite bluntly."

"We were sexually compatible, Mr. Piron, if that's what you mean." Her tone was mocking. I thought Harry must have been quite a man.

"That's not so terribly important, Gretyl, as long as the incompatibility isn't too great. I've done a lot of divorce work. That's our great stand-by. You had this thing worrying you. Usually when that happens there is friction. And, I'll put it this way, you were both dominant personalities."

Her cup tinkled on the saucer. "I wonder," she said in a low voice, "whether I was a good wife. You are right about Harry. We both liked our own way, but right from the beginning we evolved a rigid system that prevented any clash. We were reasonable. God damn it, we were civilised people."

Her face was bitter and tears welled from her eyes. "Mr. Piron, what's your first name?"

"Jim," I said. "Friends usually use plain Piron."

"Piron," she said, "there wasn't any magic about our marriage. We were gentle, courteous and considerate. Now I wish we had quarrelled occasionally. Oh, I suppose every woman wants something from marriage that doesn't exist."

"I wouldn't know. It was a long time ago." In spite of myself I felt my face stiffen.

"I'm sorry."

"No need to be."

"There's one more thing. My girl friend got in on the Tuesday morning of that week. Harry telephoned me at eight on the Monday night. He said something had come up and he maybe wouldn't be home."

"Did he say what?"

"It was part of our pattern that we didn't probe, Piron. I assumed maybe one of the papers had an emergency and Harry had agreed to work a night shift on the desk. That happened very occasionally."

I waited. "I got back from the airport at around ten. Harry was home. He was a good host, and if anything worried him he'd conceal it. I only had about half an hour with him alone. He said a friend had been in a jam and he had to help out. I thought he was embarrassed. His hands were trembling."

"Another woman?"

"I'm certain Harry hadn't another woman. That morning the only practical way to test it wasn't possible. That night I asked him if he wanted to talk about it. He said there'd be a time when he'd like to talk about it. But not then. That night he couldn't sleep."

"And that's all you know, Gretyl?"

"That's all I know." I could smell her cologne as she got up and reached for her coat.

She hesitated. "Would you like me to fix you breakfast?"

"I had it two hours ago. When you came I was doing push-ups to try to get my figure back in shape."

Her glance was all woman. "I don't think you need worry, Piron."

My palms felt sticky as I helped her on with the raincoat. I kept well away from her as I opened the door.

"Goodbye and thank you again, Piron."

I walked back to the chair on which she had been sitting. On the floor beside it was a damp newspaper. I picked it up; it was the daily morning edition of the sheet Siskin worked for.

It was folded back to one of the columns, one done by a staff man, a kind of basket for odds and ends which didn't fit in anywhere else. The par read: "Four months ago Harry Siskin, freelance writer, was found dead in a Spanish Harlem fleabag with cyanide in his brandy. Verdict, suicide. Currently the top private agency has reopened the enquiry. Developments expected soon."

I wondered why she hadn't mentioned it.

On my way to the office I took the notebook Gretyl had found to a little guy who does such work for us. Usually he gets letters written in code from sugar daddies to their popsies or the codes embezzlers use for their private ledgers. He is a retired classics teacher who lives in a little apartment crowded with books, and supplements his pay by composing deadly crossword puzzles.

He is not enthusiastic about our work, but he brightened when he saw the notebook. "Not the usual filth, Piron. Or if so, evidently educated filth. I'll call you midday."

A report was waiting for me from the handwriting expert who had returned the books from the Hotel Pablo. He was pretty sure that the same person who had signed in had signed before, on March 8th, 1970. I had the books wrapped up for return and telephoned Gould. He drawled that the three thugs were scheduled to get their comeuppance at ten, district court, and would I be present. I told him yes and got there at a quarter to the hour.

There was the usual court smell of disinfectant, furniture polish and dirty people. A very young assistant in the D.A.'s office was seated with Gould. I joined them, and a bustling little man with protruding teeth, who managed to smell of gin at this hour, came along. He was Harry Barker, who got along defending the lower echelons of crime. He was a jerky, repetitive talker.

"Morning, morning, about my three men. What say a plea to simple assault, eh?"

"I got three nice blackjacks and premeditation," drawled Gould.

"Come, come," said Barker, his eyes shrewd behind wobbly spectacles. "One of my men has a gun wound in the calf. I don't suppose Mr. Piron wants a remand and a jury, eh, eh?"

The Assistant D.A. looked at me. I was sure that somebody had handed down the suggestion to him that maybe nobody wanted to make a production number of it. I shrugged and screwed my face up.

"Okay, Barker," the D.A. said. "It's only a postponement, you know. One day those three goons are going up for a big one."

"Excellent, excellent," said Barker, scuttling away.

Presently they brought the three guys in. I gave formal evidence of being assaulted. The air was full of boredom. Barker made a little speech saying that his three clients had mistaken me for another man who had been making threats. We listened to a recital of petty convictions and each drew a month at Government expense.

It was nice to get out into the fresh air. Almost inevitably I found Gould beside me. He suggested a coffee to get the court taste out of our mouths. We found a place which catered for witnesses, policemen and guys out on bail. The coffee was good and everybody was engrossed in their private troubles.

"A funny thing happened to me this morning," said Gould, peering slyly over his cup.

"Yessir, Massah Bones, and what was that funny thing that happened to you?"

"The lieut. is a good guy. I told you last night he was sharing my curiosity about the late Mr. Siskin. Well, this morning he shuffled his papers around and said he guessed it would be a good idea not to waste any more time on it."

"That makes sense."

"There used to be a time," he said, "when a wealthy mobster, say Marcello, could stop an investigation."

"You got Marcello on the brain."

He ignored me. "But not any more. Not with homicide. So therefore I get around to doing a little figuring. I suppose you wouldn't tell me if I added it up right?"

I felt my eyes narrow. "Could be the end of the sum is a quiet little beat, say on Staten Island, for the next twenty years."

"Yeah. That was on my working sheet, too."

He put down his cup. "The way I see it personally, Piron, is that law enforcement should be left to the regular police forces. Except for maybe a little divorce creeping for guys like you. As it is, most regular forces are under strength, overworked and underpaid. No money for the cops. But if some little jerk of a filing clerk in a Government office went to a Russian friendship meeting in 1944, they'll spend twenty grand investigating him."

I got up. I wanted no part of this discussion. "So long, Gould," I said, "see you around in ten years' time."

He leered at me. "Marcello's back in town. Flew in around six this morning. Three days before schedule. Be good, baby."

While his irritating presence lingered in my mind, I found a booth and phoned a friend at headquarters. He said he would call me back and I waited around until the ring came.

"About Gould. He's a dedicated cop and he still manages to be fairly popular with the other guys. He studied nights for a law degree, and speaks good Yiddish and Spanish."

He went on to tell me that Gould had been shifted about from squad to squad and was believed to have the Inspector's eye upon him. Any day now he was slated for promotion and was tipped to go up the ladder fast. A tough, shrewd, honest cop with all the tricks of the trade.

I thanked him and hung up. For an ambitious cop a nod from the lieutenant should be good enough. Although there have been quite a few that I have known who got on remarkably quickly through looking into forbidden closets and being quietly kicked upstairs. Gould didn't quite strike me like that. I guessed I'd have a word with the Old Man and maybe with Pout.

The Old Man smoked impassively when I reported.

"That girl Siskin getting under your skin?"

"I wish she'd get under my bed linen," I told him, frankly.

"The customers are to be laid, Piron, *laid off.*"

"Sure," I said, "but let me have my dreams, guv'nor."

"So," he said, "if Siskin made a habit of going to Pablo's, the chances are that he was a private lush, a cupboard drinker. Tension in his marriage, a job that was exacting. I see a picture of a guy getting jumpy—Pout told you he was failing in his work. He couldn't drink too much in public. So periodically he has an afternoon in a fleabag with his bottle. There are worse ways."

"I have him placed as a fastidious man, sir. He'd choose a better class of hotel, I'd say."

"A lot of fastidious men—and women—like a roll in the mud occasionally. Hell, we meet it all the time. Somebody clever spots the cycle and at the psychological moment meets him in the street. 'I've got a little present for you, Harry.' The cyanide's in the bottle, and if the psychology is right it's dead sure."

He yawned. "I had a late night last night. I wanted to keep you from tangling in side issues so I put George Carter on the liquor angle. Sometimes the element of chance in investigation appals me. The police went after the source of that brandy and drew blank. The obvious place was the shopping centre nearest to Siskin's apartment.

"The liquor store is a big one, run on serve-yourself lines. You load the hooch into a trolley, and a guy takes it out to your car. Now chance comes into it to the extent that the manager went sick the day after Siskin's death and was operated on. When the police hit the store a relieving manager was in charge. He looked at the stock records and told them that this brand of hooch hadn't been in stock for a couple of years."

He chewed his cigar from side to side.

"But when George Carter hit the place, the regular manager was back on the job. A solid type of citizen. George talked to him man to man and he came through.

"Three years or so back the string of stores had experimented in stocking some high-price imported brandies. It hadn't been a success. Eventually the remaining six bottles weren't earning shelf space and went into the store-room. Two days before Siskin died the manager got sick of looking at them and dumped them in the display area marked down forty per cent. He cleared them all. And he remembers that among them were a couple of bottles of the particular brandy Siskin got the cyanide in. The stuff had long since been written off the current stock sheet."

"Maybe a coincidence," I said, a bit lamely.

"Now," the Old Man rumbled, "that day Mrs. Siskin came in and bought a fair amount of stuff. Of course, nobody remembered precisely what. The manager is positive in his identification because la Siskin had another woman with her, a petite, striking-looking brunette. Together they made a luscious picture which the manager remembered on his bed of pain."

There wasn't much to say except a muttered, "Hardly conclusive."

"I'll move the report over to Mr. Brown," he said. "To hell with it. We quit horsing around as at close of business today. Give her a negative report and two hundred of her deposit back."

On my desk was another assignment sheet and I spent the next couple of hours seeing a department-store floor manager whose inventory didn't jell. It was one of those pattern cases and before he had half finished I knew it had to be one of his two assistants and probably the better dressed of the two men I saw. I got back to the office and made the necessary arrangements. We could have cracked it in a few days, but if you do that the client queries the bill. The store was a wealthy one. We'd put three men on it for a week, dress the reports up and hear the cash register give a healthy clang. To make sure I phoned up a couple of informers I use.

At twelve the retired schoolmaster rang.

"Piron," he said, "that notebook. Whoever wrote it was a fair Latinist."

"That jells."

"Could you tell me what it's about?"

"Sorry, professor. Top secret. Maybe I shouldn't have involved you."

"I see," he said. "That's all right with me. It's in a system of contracted Latin. Most ingenious. I need maybe another eight hours and what you'll get is a free rendering. There are all sorts of gaps."

"Fine," I said, not much interested, and went back to briefing the guys who were to handle the store job.

Then I checked through a bundle of reports for a bonding company. But it was no good. A pair of green eyes and I don't know what else bothered me. I grabbed the phone and dialled her number.

"Piron," her voice was husky.

"Cook me lunch."

"Come out."

I left a note to the Old Man that some private business had come up and that I'd finalise the Siskin report first thing next morning. On the way out I called in at my apartment. At the very back of the dead luggage closet I keep a case with two good locks and a metal skin underneath the leather facing. I unlocked it and got out an old Italian point-four-four and a box of cartridges. I cleaned the gun carefully, and filled the clip. I put the gun in a briefcase.

She opened the door and I went into the warmth of the apartment. Gretyl was wearing a grey dress. I remember that tiny emerald earrings glittered beside her face.

We didn't exchange a word. I put the briefcase down and took the martini she offered me.

"Lunch in fifteen minutes." I sat and relaxed. The apartment had a peaceful atmosphere. Presently she called. In the other room a table was laid for two. I cannot recall what we ate, except that the first course was soup.

She left me to sip my second coffee while she cleared away. I put the cup down finally and went back to the living-room.

It seemed eternity until she came in and sat down.

"At least I'm dressed this time."

"Gretyl," I said, "what I'm going to say won't be pleasant hearing. First, you made a telephone call when you went up that day to collect the old lady's wallet. Secondly, the brand of peach brandy in the room where your husband died was stocked at your local liquor store on the Wednesday of the week your husband died. You made purchases in the store on that day."

I couldn't bear to look at her.

I heard her voice, monotonously level, saying, "I think I understand. I suppose a clever murderess might employ detectives. First to make her look innocent, second to see whether she had left loose ends."

There was sickness in my stomach. I heard footsteps and a soft hand raised my chin.

"But it's damned nonsense, Piron," said Gretyl Siskin and laughed so that her face lit up. I found myself on my feet, catching her under her arms and raising her up. I felt the warmth of her body and put her down immediately. It was as though the clouds had passed.

"First, the telephone call. I had an impulse to speak to Harry. I've threshed around at night half-dreaming I actually spoke to him. I called the bar they usually go to after a night shift. He wasn't there. As to the liquor store, we were scheduled to have a party on the Tuesday of the following week. I went there with my girl friend and stocked up."

"Come here." We went into the other room. Under the bar was a cupboard. She opened it and I peered at six cartons of beer, four bottles of gin, and three bottles of whisky.

"And now to the kitchen." She opened a drawer and

produced a book. Neatly annotated among other items under the date were liquor purchases. She fumbled with a spike and produced the cash register receipt with the various prices and total.

"I suppose there would be a way round," she said thoughtfully. "Suppose I bought the brandy, noted the price of something else which matched and bought it later at another store."

She smiled slowly. "I may have a murderess's mind, Piron. In many ways I'm not a nice woman. But I didn't murder Harry."

Hands on hips she faced me in challenge. Training and logic went through the window in a furtive procession of law books, training, peering through transoms, the sound of weary voices murmuring horrible little hatreds.

"I know you didn't." The words weren't adequate, but she caught my hand and pressed it to her.

"Come on, I've got more coffee."

This time we sat on two small stools and sipped coffee and drank brandy.

"I wish we had a fire," she said presently, "instead of central heating. I remember when I was a child in Oregon . . ."

"We had big wood fires, too," I said, and we shared a common memory.

The companionable minutes went by too quickly.

"What now—about the case?" she asked.

I told her the Old Man was quitting at close of business.

"Piron, there are times when I realise I'm an obstinate bitch. I know you well enough to know you've enquired about me."

"I met a guy you worked with."

Her laugh was golden-bronze. "I think I know who you mean. He said I ride horses to death, I expect. So I do. It's a habit I am going to quit. I'm trying to analyse about Harry. I was certain he didn't suicide, the calm acceptance that he did infuriated me. What I was proving I frankly don't know." Her eyes met mine levelly. "His other job was mostly routine, one of those long, dull roads where you drive along half-dozing and suddenly there's a dangerous corner. If it's better—considering his other job—to let it lie, then I quit, too."

I said quietly, "I've got some leave of absence piled up. The last six months I've led a dog's life. No overtime pay, but a backlog of time I can take off. I would have racked up close on a month. I thought of taking it from tomorrow and looking around on my own."

Her eyes thanked me. Aloud she said, "Piron, may I leave the decision to you? Oh, God, I don't want to make another decision ever." She got to her feet, stretching on her long legs.

The air seemed to crackle. I found myself clutching her and felt her thighs arch towards me. I bent down and lifted her and heard her voice, thick, coming from far off. "Not here, Jim. Not here."

I put her down and she clutched the arm of a chair. Sweat pricked my chest.

"My place?"

Her head was bent so that I could only see the coppery hair. She was shuddering and shaking her head.

I sat down, rubbery legged.

"I'll get a drink." She was a long time and when she came back she had put on new make-up, not that she wore much, and looked cool and fresh.

She had a long botttle in her hand. "I meant this for lunch. Forgot."

The label said it was a Niersteiner 1954.

"Handle that reverently," I said, "better let me open it." It was too chilled. I opened it and let it stand.

"That's a fine wine," I said.

"I bought it for Harry in a mad moment. Cost the earth."

"Gretyl," I said, feeling old. "I'm a red-haired middle-aged private detective. I've been in too many sweaty beds, listened to too many things."

"Hush," she said, "you're a man named Piron."

Presently the wine was gone and we talked. I learned a

lot about her. As for me, there were too many reticences, too many pretences, barricades against memory.

The light began to fade.

"Gretyl," I said, "sixty miles out is a motel. A nice place with trees around."

Her back was turned. "I'll go and pack," she said.

She changed into a skirt and sweater, and held a medium-sized travelling case.

"Put that down." Very gently I kissed her. Her breath seemed very sweet to me. I caught sight of the briefcase I had brought and started to laugh.

I sat down. "Your janitor and his brothers!"

"Schultz. What about him?"

"Guardian angels, watching over you."

"Police?"

"Kind of hush-hush ones."

"Oh."

"Do you mind?"

"Piron, if I want to sleep with a man, I don't care who knows."

I nodded. "That's what I thought, Gretyl. One more thing. If the murderer gets pressed, he may try to kill you."

She whitened slightly. I dug out the forty-four. "Any knowledge of guns?"

"I had a boy friend once years ago, who was mad on them. He taught me. I've got one he gave me." She went out, and returned with a little fancy mother-of-pearl, lady's pistol of the type which are, maybe, some good if the target keeps very still and you are two feet away.

"It's loaded," she said. "When Harry was out nights I felt better with it in the bedroom."

"Leave that one for little girls," I said. "This is my private stock, unregistered. I took it off a nasty fellow who isn't around any more. There's a bullet in the spout. You just lift the safety catch and press. The bullets come out until you've exhausted the clip or stop pressing. Aim low and to the left. The recoil will raise the barrel up and to the right."

She didn't shudder or go in for girlish tricks, just tried its feel and flinched slightly under the weight. "Just a minute."

She came back with a handbag that fixed over her shoulder on a long strap. It was heavy leather, intaglioed into a lot of monkey faces.

"It's a horrible thing, doesn't go with anything. A present from an amorous city editor who'd vacationed in Cairo. The first time I've worn it, but it's just the thing for Two-Gun Annie."

"Gretyl," I said, "I'm serious. Whoever it is is cunning. Don't answer the door to strange men, or strange women."

"If I don't," she said with direct frankness, "he or she won't be caught."

I couldn't think of an answer.

We used her four-year-old car. The weather had improved sufficiently for the cool dampness of the air to be pleasant on my skin. The road flowed softly beneath the wheels.

She unpacked while I showered. My suit was bearing up but I wished I had a change. I went into the bar and waited. She wore a shimmering jade green semi-formal. It looked like silk to me, but she gave a superior woman-giggle and told me it was some tongue-twisting synthetic.

"Unlike you."

"That's nice, Piron." She raised her glass to me.

It was a nice place, and expensive, and therefore discreet. You find discretion in the top or lowest bracket, a discreet head waiter or a discreet flop-house keeper with scars on his face. Between is suspicion, between is nosiness. It was too early in the year to dine outside, a feature of the place, but indoors it had been arranged with a charming, half-mocking rusticity. The service was soft-footed and perfect, the food superb. I mused about the cost, maybe, of keeping a woman. She was the kind that you wanted to have nice things. I guessed I could hit the Old Man for a hefty raise. I never bothered much, disliking those knock-'em-down and throw-'em-out hasslings which pass for wage negotiation in the

Big City. Or I could go back to practising law. A big firm, the kind that handle million-dollar estates and are filled with prematurely old young men brooding over income-tax law, had hinted I might have a humble job dealing with bastardy cases and other pranks that wealthy young wards and beneficiaries involve themselves in.

I signed the bill and suggested a walk. We wandered among the pines. The air was soft and sweet. Presently we got back to the cabin, carefully suggestive of rough logs on the outside and inches deep in carpet on the inside. I wondered about the state of my wallet. Not baseball, Piron, to borrow from the lady.

"I packed a spare toothbrush for you." She smiled and carried a dressing-gown into the bathroom. I sat on an overstuffed chair and looked at my watch. Eleven o'clock. The ideal time for love. I went over and tested the bed. Pneumatic softness. A door opened behind me.

I watched her walk over to her case. She dumped stuff in it and straightened up. Her face, usually mobile, was strained, almost ugly, if she could have been. The bones gave the illusion of standing out under thick white skin.

"I can't, Piron." Her voice was drained.

"That's all right," I could hear my voice, harsh and unyielding, although I did not will it to be so. "But you'll hate yourself in the morning."

"Jim, don't be smart, for God's sake!"

"I'm sorry." I took the case. "You better take the car."

"Look," she said, "I'll drive out first thing and collect you."

I took the bag outside and dropped it on the back seat. "Don't worry," I said, "there's a big notice about hire cars over the desk. I'll return in state like MacArthur, only not as a conqueror."

There was a hint of a wry grin on her pallor. I was glad she didn't keep saying she was sorry, as some women will. I watched her start the motor. I poked my head through the window.

"One thing, phone me when you get back."

For an instant her lips fluttered against mine and then I was watching the tail lights of the car. I walked back into the very empty cabin. Presently I went out and found a bright little guy in buttons. Money passed and he came back with an incurious look and a bottle of brandy.

When her call came through, the bottle was half empty. I was standing, feeling my chin stubbly against the top of my shirt, giving myself a rambling lecture about self-sufficient Jim Piron. The words came out rather mashed through stale lips. I lurched to the phone.

"I'm back, Jim, I drove slowly."

"Lock the front door!"

"I have, Jim. Thank you. I think we had better not meet again."

"Lock the front door!" I could hear my thick breath and the liquor-spread width of the vowels. I got the handset back on the rest. Then the bed tilted up and hit me. I felt the heavy wooden shelves at the back crash against my face, had the momentary impression my legs were flying in the air, and then came black easement.

A huckster once told me cars are phallic symbols, which didn't add up with my memories: T-model Fords, which I equated with a beat-up old broad trundling her stomach around waterfront bars. Maybe he was right. A bashed-down ego put me in a Cadillac with a sardonic little driver. On the way I stopped at a barber-shop and a place which pressed pants and a haberdashery shop where I bought a shirt. When I paid it all off I had eighty-five cents.

The barber's mirror and the sting of his styptic pencil showed me the cuts and a new, greenish bruise on the right cheek-bone where I'd hit my face on the bed.

It was eleven fifteen when I came scowling into the office. There was a pile of messages on my file. I lifted up the portable, and made out a bill for Mrs. Gretyl Siskin, for three hundred dollars. I enclosed the rebate cheque which was in my file, and wrote a brief report on the company's letterhead. "We regret that we have no further evidence concerning this case." I signed it and dragged out a private, plain sheet of paper. I destroyed the first, and the second, while the little pickaxes knocked inside my head. What I finally wrote was: "Gretyl. The boy will wait for a receipt. For God's sake, this is total surrender. Are there any terms at all?"

The boy, young Sylvester, is a small eye-apple of mine. If native cunning, guts and a brain that assimilates facts like blotting-paper constitute criteria, the lad will end up as a rather good private eye. Usually we josh. Today he was solemnly stolid. "My boy," I said, producing money, "you will hire a taximeter cabriolet, avoiding the temptation to go by bus and pocket the difference, and take this. Wait for a receipt."

I waited for the pungent answer. "Yessir," he said, wheeled, and marched, and then the Old Man's secretary buzzed that the Presence had need of me. It was typical of him that he didn't ask questions. Although, of course, he never does while you're braced for them.

We worked through a file of fourteen new divorce cases, some of them tricky, and talked over methods. To my relief I was saddled with none of them. He put them aside, and drew out a Bonding Company assignment. There was a guy in line for a thirty-thousand-dollar job who had a couple of no-good brothers. I saw from the notes that he was obviously in the clear, but bonding companies don't take chances.

"No hurry," said the Old Man. "Maybe you start tomorrow."

It would mean a quick trip to maybe four cities, enough to keep me out of town for a week. In his way, he's an understanding old devil. Trouble is to work out how much he understands.

When I returned to my desk, the code expert was waiting for me. It was the first time I had ever seen him in the office. I had the impression that his feet never took him farther than the nearest reference library. He was a frail old guy with a head too big for his thin neck. He peered at me over his glasses.

"I thought it was perhaps urgent, so I brought it along."

It had gone completely out of my mind. Forcing myself to forget my throbbing skull and nauseated stomach, I took the insignificant little book and the sheet of foolscap covered with angular handwriting.

"I should say that the man who wrote it had a working acquaintance with a couple of the Romance languages. He used very contracted Latin and quite a few obscure allusions. Very interesting. A lot of my translation is guesswork."

The professor had padded the notebook out to around six hundred words, with footnotes explaining classical allusions, which my aching brain could not follow.

When the specks in the air settled down sufficiently, I read it carefully. It was as if the dead man had talked to himself on paper, giving himself a safety valve during time of crisis when he couldn't talk to anybody else. There was one passage I fastened on which made some sense to me :

Is it a trap? Feel I have gone on too long and strayed too far. G. anxious for me to go back to a newspaper desk. Wonder if at my age I could get the breaks. Tension between G. and me is palpable. I feel I am failing her. I finally took the plunge and placed a bait for G.L. I don't know how he took it, if at all. Marcello very difficult. I doubt whether S. really knows as much as she hints.

I thanked him. He was curious and I shut him off. A nice little man, but I didn't like mankind *in toto* that morning.

Sylvester came back with an envelope. Inside was a receipt and a small piece of paper. Her writing was large, clear and free-flowing. More of a man's writing, it seemed to me. "Perhaps after a year if we both feel so."

"She was a nice lady. Gave me a slice of pie," observed Sylvester.

"That's all, my boy." He scuttled out.

I had a couple of things to do in connection with the inventory shortage at the store. It occurred to me I should give Siskin's notebook to Pout. I hadn't included it in the report. I telephoned his home. A polite negative voice said that Mr. Pout would call me back shortly. In five minutes his deep voice was on the wire.

"I've got something for you," I said. "Could I see you?" We fixed it at his apartment in an hour, which just left me time to pay my two calls. The pain in my head localised, but my stomach was still sick and my hands greasy and trembling.

Pout was five minutes late. I stood in his study and admired his collection of fishing rods. It was an elegant place in bachelor style.

"Hallo." I thought he eyed me somewhat quizzically. Of course, he'd know of my little excursion with Gretyl but he was much too good a gentleman to allude to it.

I gave him the book and the translation and explained where I got it. He studied the two documents methodically for half an hour.

"Who did this?"

I told him. "I know of him," he grunted, "and admire his crosswords. On my bright days I manage to do maybe seven per cent of the clues. Hm."

He exuded force and concentration as he eyed me. "You know, Piron, it was naughty of you not to put it in a report and equally naughty of you not to have handed over the book when you found it."

My stomach fluttered and I gave him a deeper scowl than I intended and saw his eyes narrow as if he were calculating something.

"Pout," I said, "this isn't one of my bright days. Give me a break. I don't want to be lectured on duty by you or anyone."

His expression switched to solicitude. "I'm a rotten host, would you like a drink?"

"If you have anything for a brandy hangover, yes."

He was gone about five minutes. The beaker he handed me was dark and slightly frothing. I took a swig and it burned inside. I finished it in sips. My stomach and head became quieter and sweat burst out on my forehead. He grinned. "I occasionally have recourse to it. I can't tell you the recipe. It's a secret of my man's."

"I'm already much better," I said. "The minor miracle class. I'm sorry I reacted sharply, but at the time I didn't think there was anything to it and I still don't."

He massaged his chin and looked absently at the old hunting prints on the wall.

"What it does tell is that Siskin was breaking down. I wouldn't have thought it. I even reckoned I was being a little hard when I advised Brown to take him off outside work. He was rambling to himself. I don't understand it all, but there are a couple of obscure allusions to cases he'd worked on over the past two years." He puffed his cheeks out and shook his head.

"There's a reference to Marcello and a guy named G.L."

"Yes. The man we reckon might be changing hot money through Marcello sometimes goes by the name of George Long. A baddie from way back, if he's who we think he is. Maybe we'll pull him in this week."

"Okay, that clears my interest in the case."

He smiled. "I'm afraid that the evidence of the liquor store made up my mind. Mrs. Siskin. Poor woman, in a way, but smart the way she turned Siskin's neurosis against him. It'll never be proved."

He asked me to stay to lunch. There was steak, and his man had a certain way with Sauce Robert which gave it an added piquancy. I'd become quite fond of J. R. P. Pout on our short acquaintance. But I wasn't in the mood for company and he showed me out.

There was a mirror in his hallway. I caught sight of my face and experienced a slight sense of shock. My face seemed to have shrunk back on the skull beneath, and the barber had cut my hair shorter than I wanted. Two sick, burning eyes stared out of their sockets. It was a killer's face. I felt ashamed.

In the weak sunshine I felt better. Pout's potion had left me feeling rather stunned. The pain had backed away into tiny corners, but I had a feeling of unreality. I felt my head was too close to the pavement as though I had shrunk. Suddenly I thought of the mixed grills at Dick's Bar and felt hungry. I took a taxi and got there around two.

I ordered a cold beer and forced myself to drink it. It was like vitriol and I went into the men's room and was sick. I came back and ordered another. This was better and I started to feel a little human.

Dick came up and looked at me in embarrassment, and even fear when I looked closely at him.

"It's okay about the other night, Dick," I said, "but you owe me a favour for one of these fine days." It was better that way. As I had played it I had one fat publican on a little string.

I ordered my mixed grill with sundry elaborations. He vanished through the door into the kitchen and presently came back.

"I've got a peep window so I can always watch the bar," he said.

"Common practice, Richard."

"And now I pay you back that favour." He wet his lips. "The dame who used to come in with the man whose picture you showed me. She's just gone into the fourth booth down. She's wearing a red coat."

The detective got the better of the man, who just wanted kidneys, lamb chops, ham, steak, mushrooms, french fried potatoes on a plate—and maybe a little garlic toast.

"This the first time she's been in for months?"

He shrugged. "I think so, as far as nights go. During the day I've got an uncle, a retired barkeeper, who takes my place most times. He's sick today."

I walked past the booth and stopped. Leaning in I said pleasantly, "Excuse me if I'm wrong. But I think you knew a friend of mine." I flipped his photograph, now worn at the edges from my wallet, onto the table beside her drink.

Her lack-lustre blue eyes looked listlessly down and I saw her start. "My God, you know Paul?" Her voice was one of those with a tiny whine to it. I put down my glass of beer and sat down.

As I forced a smile onto my face I studied her. Expensively groomed, although daily massage could not erase the tell-tale wrinkles round the eyes and incipient flabbiness of the neck. Her features were pleasantly regular and she could have been very pretty once. I knew the type. A hard-drinking good-time girl in her youth who gets out with a big bankroll and no future except gin rummy and a bottle.

"Where is Paul?" Her voice was soft and eager. For the time being my sudden appearance in her life did not strike her as odd : presently it would. There was sharp shrewdness now in her eyes.

"He's dead." She slumped a little, then straightened up. A battler.

"Excuse me?" It was Dick who walked up with that fancy-footed stealth you note with many overweight characters. "Could I see you a minute?"

"You'll wait?" I looked at the woman.

"You bet I'll wait." Her voice was without the whining, tinny note I'd noted.

I followed Dick through the flap in the bar and into the kitchen. It smelled agreeably savoury. My mouth watered as I saw my grill fizzling on the grill over the glowing charcoal bed.

"Favour returned," said Dick, "and a bonus. One of the guys at the bar is an old-timer on a theatrical paper. I asked him if he knew the woman. She's a Mrs. Sybil Green. A lot of dough."

"Thanks," I said, still eyeing the grill.

His hand detained me.

"God, Piron, with you it's all drink, women and mixed grills. I may be risking something telling you this."

I looked into his shrewd, world-weary eyes and said, "I'll owe you a favour if you've got anything."

His round mouth whispered at me, "That woman was the original Miss Bumps. Sure, before you got to this town maybe. The first of the big-time strippers, just about. 'Miss Bumps' they called her and it was true. She hooked an oil guy named Green. He was dead in nine months. They say she was that sort of girl. But he left her half a million and that was in 1934. Now what do you know about Marcello?"

"Not much. They call him the Big Fish around town, and he wears cuff links with fish on 'em."

"In 1945 he's small-time, but he comes up fast. Sure, he's good, but he starts by buying Old Paddy Moynihan's bookie connection. That takes dough. You don't walk in, muscles or not. You got to have connections and dough. So it's Miss Bumps' dough he uses. He's maybe four years younger and, of course, when he's established Miss Bumps is out."

Now my mind was alert. I pressed his shoulder and went back.

"How did he die?" Her glass was empty and I beckoned the waiter. She ordered gin and water. I put another beer on the tab.

"The story is," I said carefully, "that he went into a better class of flea-bag with a bottle of peach brandy, put cyanide in it and took a glass. Verdict, suicide. A few months ago."

Her eyes were narrow. "You a detective?"

"Private, for the insurance company. Routine."

"How did you know me?"

"Hawking his photograph round bars on my flat feet." I was playing it the flashy way. I wanted her to place me as a cheap low-grade snooper. She gave me a glance of appraisal. I made my face stupid and blank and was thankful I hadn't changed my suit. It was rumpled and one lapel was badly stained where the brandy had slopped.

"Was it suicide?"

"Maybe." I made the word come out flat.

"The bastard!" The epithet hissed between her teeth, involuntarily.

I looked slightly startled. She controlled herself. I saw the effort.

"He wasn't the type to drink alone in flop-houses." She said that less to help me than to justify herself.

My mixed grill arrived. Without asking her permission I

started to eat greedily. It was no effort. As I ate, savouring the juiciness of the meat and the pungent sauce, and the french fries crisp on the outside and melting into genial flouriness as one's teeth bit in, I felt her studying me.

"Mr. uh . . ."

"Jack South, ma'am. I'll give you a card in a minute." I sopped up the remainder of the sauce with my bread. I finished and allowed myself the luxury of a slight belch. It was a pity I had on a clean shirt, but I'd managed to loosen it at the collar.

"And what might be your name, ma'am?"

"Mrs. Sybil Green."

I produced a notebook and pencil and wrote her name down in big letters.

"Look," she said, "could we talk at my apartment?"

"That's all right with me, ma'am." I looked cunning. "I'm afraid I don't get taxi fare."

She said that was all right and I pretended to be tying up my shoe-lace when she picked up my tab.

Her apartment echoed with the sweet chime of gold pieces and a good decorator with a free hand into the money bags. Nothing was out of place. The only other person I could see around was a squat woman with a wart on her nose who looked as though she might have been a theatrical dresser some time. She glanced at me with disapproval. I sat on the edge of an imported cane *chaise longue* with my hat nervously perched on my knees. I ran my hands down its beautifully woven sides and admired the superb simplicity of its design. Next year it would probably be junked and another fashion substituted.

I watched her walk over to a sideboard. She was still straight-backed on her high heels. She walked with the free striding grace which possession of great beauty can give and which is never lost. Her figure had gone and the veins in one leg were badly knotted. But she still had something.

"A drink, Mr. South?"

"Sure, uh, I don't drink much on duty. But maybe say a little Scotch."

I sipped it greedily. She'd poured around half a tumblerful.

"I met Paul Harding around eight months ago," her voice had the whine back underneath. "I was standing watching them destroying a rather nice old house not far from here and he asked me if I knew its history. As I hope you've gathered, I'm not in the habit of picking up men." Her empty eyes flickered around the room.

"Sure, no, madam," I scuffed my feet into the pile carpet of eggshell blue.

"We got into the habit of having a drink together two or three times a week, maybe, always at the place you saw me in. He never came here, we never met anywhere else. He'd phone me. I knew he was a journalist, I knew he was bitterly unhappy at home. We had a lot in common."

Clever Harry, I thought—the real professional touch.

"What did you talk about?" I asked dully.

"Oh, life, New York. Sometimes we didn't need to talk much at all. I'm sorry I can't help you more. I never even knew where he lived. We agreed not to pry."

Like hell, I said inwardly, looking at her sharp, avid mouth.

She started to pump me, mostly about his wife. I looked cunning. "Of course, I'd pay your expenses," she suggested skilfully.

I gave a fair imitation of a man torn between a steady ill-paid job and maybe a five-hundred-dollar bonus. In the end I produced a greasy card with the fake name on it and the backing of an impenetrable accommodation address. She was experienced enough to let the fish dangle on the hook a little longer. I said I'd telephone her next day and shambled out into the elevator.

There wasn't enough traffic in her expensive backwater to inhibit parking entirely. I found a cabbie and asked him to wait. Presently a smart chauffeur-driven car came up to the apartment house and Mrs. Green got into it. I told the cabbie to follow. In a downtown section he slowed right down before a drab-looking building and I saw her get out.

I let the cab pass and go another hundred yards before I stopped. I tipped him well.

As he shifted into first, he kept the clutch in. "Mister," he said, "that building houses a company called Social Enterprises." He laughed as he said the name. "You heard of a guy named Marcello? It's his."

I looked dumb.

"So I shouldn't hang around, mister!" He let in the clutch.

Opposite was a quick-lunch place, dowdy as the rest of the street. In a way I wasn't surprised to see Gould slumped on a stool in the corner. I sat beside him and got the favour of his grin.

"As soon as I saw you and the dame go into her apartment, I got out here by bus. I expected you to take longer. Losing the old s.a., Piron?"

"I thought you were off the Siskin business?" He'd neatly trapped me. I cursed myself and he knew it.

"It's like this, I've got two, three days off. I thought I might do worse than follow you around. You surely looked like hell this morning when you got in. I thought you were sick. In a paddy, too."

"You can't annoy me." My head had started to ache again, a dull pound at the back of the skull.

"I was a bit hasty, Piron, yesterday. If you've got a cloak-and-dagger angle it doesn't interest me. But I've got a hunch. I tell myself a good cop doesn't have hunches. It's his feet, his analytical mind and maybe a little rough stuff that gets the cases on the blotter. But this hunch is one luxury I'll allow."

He ran a hand through his thinning fair hair and tried his old trick of a stiff-fingered jab to the breast bone. I was watching for it and slapped his hand down.

He peered at me. "You look fairly tough today, Piron. However, what I was saying is that my hunch is that you'll lead me to Marcello."

I needed his knowledge so I just shrugged. "How does Sybil Green fit into Marcello's life, Gould?"

He leered. "Social Enterprises! I must tell you that Marcello's got a sense of humour, and although I hate his guts I admit it's a good one. Social Enterprises. Built on the numbers game, rigged races, dope, and a string of whorehouses throughout the country. That was years ago. The houses, the numbers, and maybe the dope have gone. Now it's a big holding company for industrial shares, a staff of analysts employed, all that. The story is that Sybil owns forty-two per cent, Marcello forty-two per cent, and a firm of attorneys holds the odd sixteen points."

"Sybil must be wealthy."

He nodded and dragged at his cigarette.

"Sixteen years ago Marcello's a hood, one of those good-looking muscle-boys in an Italian way. Romantic-looking, hard underneath. Miss Bumps is four years older. She falls for Marcello. He uses her money to start big. In 1955 Miss Bumps, what with the gin and late nights hasn't got much to show any more. So out she goes."

"I can't understand . . ."

He finished it for me. "Why she didn't end up in the East River. There are guys who point to that fact as denoting Marcello's magnanimity. Other guys say that she had the best attorneys in town, and in their safe is a complete record of her ex-lover's capers. And just to be sure, photostat copies in a couple of safe deposits. So she gets forty-two per cent of what the holding company makes."

"A shrewd gal."

He nodded. "That's what the record shows. A little floosie from Indiana who promoted what she had into big business. But she hasn't got Marcello."

"That riles her."

"They have to see each other over business. They worked out a kind of agreement, but when she's drunk she hates Marcello and maybe takes a cab over to rile him. She drunk now?"

I shook my head.

"Pity."

I said, "The interesting thing is that Marcello's so big. I'd only heard of him."

"You know how it goes. It's difficult for a crumb to get out of the rackets. A lot of his activities are legitimate. But apart from the profit, he likes the other side."

"And nobody knows where he went to school."

"You mean when they tried to deport him, though they didn't get to first base?" He laughed. "I've met Marcello a few times. I haunt him a bit, just for the hell of it, and maybe the hope he'll give me a legit. excuse to smash his bridge work. He's got mad a couple of times and—do you know what?—he lapsed into Pennsylvania Dutch. The quaint idioms and all. I come from there and know it like the back of my hand. I guess when his parents died some suckers from there took him in. He probably got them insured and had them knocked off."

I peered out of the door. Sybil Green's car still stood there. I yawned. "I'm through, Gould, going home. This time you pick up the tab. If you go after me you'll only get pneumonia."

I walked two blocks and got a cab. The headache had vanished somewhere among my dislike of Gould. I heard my voice giving the address of the Siskin apartment. Something inside, maybe a vestigial conscience, was trying to yell "no". But only the Siskin address emerged.

I got there at around six forty-five, after the cabbie had battled through the traffic. His face in the mirror said it was my fault. I undertipped him and then relented. His face told me I was a piker.

I rang the bell. The round-faced little woman who'd opened the door stood there, her mouth pursed and vague horror peeping through her glasses. I watched her scuttle away and wondered if she could speak.

Gretyl wore a little number that my bloodshot eyes registered as turquoise. Her stockings were tan. I noticed because I couldn't look at her face.

"Come in." There was a soft undertone of humour. "And

Piron," I met her eyes, "this ain't gonna do you the slightest good, buster."

"Just a suppliant, faint with hunger and a brandied stomach."

"I don't know about your stomach, but I can smell it on your suit. Piron, are you hopeless? Don't you know about women and good cigars, for God's sake." We stood and looked at each other, until a rustling noise came from the little woman. She was introduced as Mrs. Syme or Aunt Chrissie, a sort of distant relation who happened to live in the district.

"And Aunt," said Gretyl, "never never leave me alone with Piron. He has intentions against my virtue."

Surprisingly, the little woman grinned. If a gargoyle had commenced to sing in a soprano voice it couldn't have flabbergasted me more.

"You'd better take a bath," said Gretyl, critically. "It might help." She sounded doubtful. "And leave that filthy coat here." I obeyed and wallowed in her bath. I thought of her in it, and reached up and turned the cold shower on.

I took my time and came back to the faint smell of cleaning fluid. She had an apron on and looked business-like. My wallet and cigarettes were on a small table. "I've hung it out," she said. I noticed that the big leather bag was slung on the back of a chair. She followed my glance.

"Oh, I'm taking your advice. And the janitor's brother leered at me when I went out shopping. I felt it."

Auntie shuttled in, looked and retreated to the kitchen. "You're doing fine," Gretyl called after her.

Suddenly we were grinning at each other foolishly. I gestured an interrogation towards the kitchen.

"She knows. Not about last night though. She's sleeping here. Not only to deliver me from temptation, but because she's a dead shot, or so I've heard."

"Now Gretyl, I've seen Mr. E. Hoover. A master of disguise perhaps, but I doubt, I very much doubt, if he is Auntie Chrissie."

I listened to her golden laugh, relishing it.

"Piron, you weren't born in New York. Neither was I. I forget the percentage who were. Harry once did an article about it." Her voice trailed away and my nerves twanged like a plucked violin. Her pause was momentary. "Auntie Chrissie—her father was my father's great-cousin—spent sixty years in Arizona. Her husband managed a small ranch. She's got just enough to live on and she came here because it fascinates her. New Yorkers like you make her nervous. But she can amputate a finger, drench a cow and when necessary use a gun on a snake."

I whistled. I decided I'd tell her about Sybil Green over dinner. The meal was simple and she apologised for its smallness.

"Woman diet, Piron. That's a great fact of life and maybe a misery. Women alone pick at little egg dishes."

I was enjoying eggs poached in burgundy and onion and spread over bread crisply fried in butter.

Presently I got to the last of the French-style pancakes, the almond paste crisp inside.

"About your husband's death," I started to say.

Aunt Chrissie's voice, the first time I'd heard it, was surprisingly gruff for a little woman. "Let it lay." Her eyes flickered at Gretyl. "What are you trying to prove? You were a goodish wife, but you were bad for each other."

She drank her coffee stolidly while I told about Mrs. Green. "So Harry was prying around Marcello. If he has got a weak link she's it. And she thought, in the first shock, that Marcello killed Harry."

I concentrated upon the coffee. Gretyl was nibbling at a knuckle of her left hand. A small diamond cluster glinted on her ring finger.

"Woman like that," said Aunt Chrissie, "would get mad, particularly after she'd been drinking. When she sobered up she'd think of the money, maybe go to Marcello."

Her bland eyes surveyed me. She was a smart woman. I made a mental note to take a closer look at old ladies in future.

"Your aunt's right in one way, Gretyl. Sooner or later

things will catch up with Marcello. The world's shoved forward a bit since Capone. For him it'll be either gaol, most probably, or a bullet out of the past."

"What kind of a man is he?" Her voice was faraway.

"Physically? Running to fat now, not unattractive to women. And if you have the slightest idea of trying to investigate him yourself, I'll tell you that you wouldn't stand a chance." My voice was madder than maybe it had any right to be.

"I suppose he has a girl friend," Gretyl said. I damned well knew that she knew.

"He doesn't change around like lesser fry, Gretyl, such as private detectives. I'd describe him as fundamentally monogamous." I sipped my wine and leered a little as she looked at the tablecloth. Auntie was peering into her coffee cup as though she saw a Dark Stranger there.

"The current monog," I pressed Gretyl's knee under the table, "has been monogged for nigh on two years. A lifetime for a guy named Marcello. He hates her, can't leave her."

Afterwards we sat in her lounge and we talked for a time. Aunt Chrissie said nothing unless she had a definite point to make. In spite of the janitor I felt happier because of her presence. At about ten I put my coat on. It smelled of the cleaning compound but the stain was gone.

"I suppose," I said to Auntie, "there'd be no point in my trying to persuade you to go to a late film show?"

Her round eyes surveyed me solemnly. "Not a chance."

I stretched and yawned. "Then I'll be going in a minute. I feel I haven't slept for a week." It was pleasant to sit peacefully in this room with my loved one. Auntie, bless her, took my hint and the coffee cups into the kitchen.

When I had seated myself on the arm of her chair she asked, "What kind of a woman is Marcello's girl?"

I told her about the pansy-blue eyes, the fair hair and the curves.

"You saw her?"

"I saw her."

"And you spent the night with her."

"Mostly she was teaching me speciality dancing."

"Mostly. And do you think she would be better than I?"

I looked down into the little amber flecks in her green eyes and gently kissed her.

"I'm a sucker for titillàtion, my pet, but I think I'll go home."

Her hand told me, "Come again."

I left her in the chair. Auntie came with me to the door.

"Mr. Piron," she said gruffly. "I have a great regard for Gretyl. I only ask you one thing. Be very certain in your own mind. She's not every man's kind of woman and she's been hurt."

There was a light on in the janitor's quarters. I wondered if they had bugged Gretyl's apartment. I thought probably yes.

It was a soft spring night and I walked along the suburban streets. On this occasion it seemed the world of Marcello was very strange and far away: also the world of spymasters, of microfilms in strange places. Coincidentally my glance fixed on a large crack in the concrete of the wall I was passing. For no reason I squatted down on my haunches and inserted two fingers. A spider ran up my wrist and an old, atavistic horror caused me to shake my arm quickly. It ran back up the wall and into its cave. Happy spider.

I straightened up. Five yards behind me, frozen against the wall, was a uniformed cop, indecision on his face. I walked quickly away. When I had gone maybe thirty yards I risked a glance back. There he was squatting down peering suspiciously at the hole. Even a spider has no privacy these days.

Meanness and a feeling of lassitude made me use public transport home. I tumbled straight into bed.

It was midnight when the telephone extension on the table roused me. Strangely for me I came awake immediately.

A grating urgent voice, "Sammy B. here."

It was my private code identification for a little man named Duggan. He's a small-time fence. In his line of business he picks up small parcels of compact objects which have been stolen and peddles them to his hand-picked list of barmen. They in turn spot old customers who have no objection to buying, say, a small electric drill for fifty per cent off the store price. The guy who did the stealing would collect maybe fifteen per cent of the take, the big fence would work in thirty, Duggan and the barman haggled out the rest. He made a nice living and was an informer on the side.

Most stuff that is stolen is by way of amateurs. They don't know where to go, and, by the time they find out that most pawnbrokers are honest and a lot have private lines to the nearest precinct house, it's too late. But some of the bigger fences find the amateur. A man in debt to loan sharks who's in a position to steal certain classes of goods quite often gets a proposition. Sometimes he is in no position to argue.

I had reckoned that this was the case with the store inventory I had on my file. One of the people I had contacted was Duggan.

I grabbed a pencil and note-book.

"Okay, Duggan."

"About that cutlery steal."

"Sure."

"What did you say was in it for me?"

I'd said a hundred dollars. I reiterated it.

"I think it's worth more, maybe two." He had a rather soft, dogged little voice. Tonight it sounded nervous. I put it down to his attempt to jack up the price.

"Duggan," I said. "It's one of two guys. A couple of days checking and we've got him."

We settled at a hundred and ten. He asked me to meet him at a bar where he usually hung out. There was a third party involved. I made it clear that Duggan would have to pay whoever it was.

I sighed and looked at the clock. Tomorrow I'd have

a lot of cleaning up to do if I was slated to catch a plane out of town sometime in the afternoon.

"Okay," I said. "You'll get your money later. I haven't got that much."

That was agreeable. He told me not to park my car outside the bar. I snorted at him, hung up and got some nondescript clothes out of the closet.

My car, paid for by the office, was three years old and looked shabby. I cursed the late traffic and inched along. The bar I was going to was in an old warehouse district which still hung on because of its proximity to the docks. Eventually I left the traffic behind, the theatre-goers yawning comfortably and guessing the second act was dull, the night owls coming in to the bright lights, the half-drunks frantically gripping the wheel and concentrating.

The street with the bar in it was a smelly canyon, deserted at night, except for a few watersiders coming off shift, and watchmen. The bar I was going to catered for them, a gloomy place, with an atmosphere of hopelessness, an ideal habitat for Duggan.

One side of it was against a man-made cliff, some forty feet high. Along the top ran another parallel street. Therefore the old buildings had their top floors projecting up and above the upper street. While the basements and bottom floors remained engaged during the day in the gloomy dullness of bulk stores and specialised warehouses, the upper storeys fronted onto a street several strata better class.

At this level an enterprising development syndicate had spruced the buildings up, providing separate entrances for offices and shops. It reminded me of a barman I knew. The area of him visible to the public was spruce, even dapper. By chance I discovered that the white, immaculate shirt-front and monkey jacket terminated in filthy old trousers and broken-down old shoes doubtless encasing unwashed feet.

This night the street looked completely deserted. The lighting was bad. It was the place for dirty thoughts and mean deeds, a scrabbling, nail-bitten street getting a living as best it could. I carefully locked the car and walked a few yards. Suddenly I found myself on my knees, dry-mouthed. My knuckles hurt me for a fraction of a second before I felt the numbed pain behind my ear. I heard running feet. Then the blackjack came again.

When I recovered consciousness I kept my eyes closed. I could feel a swelling behind my ear throbbing gently. Then I noticed a peculiar and horrible smell and couldn't place it.

The place had a foetid atmosphere. I sat propped against something and was sick. My left wrist hurt numbly. It felt swollen.

"Snap out of it. Piron." The voice was boring, insistent. I blinked into a weak, pallid light and the face of Gould. The grinning mask was gone. My brain registered the fact that his sharp features could be pleasing to look at.

"Take just a little time." I blinked around, the facts registering slowly. It appeared to be a basement. A couple of twenty-watt lights blinked nakedly overhead. In the cavernous depth were some benches and piles of what looked like material. I got it. An old clothes depository. Charities collect them, deliver them at a per weight price to the warehouses, where they are picked over. The best find their way to second-hand dealers, the others are unpicked to be pulped for paper. An old trade which prosperity and synthetics slowly reduces. Near at hand was an area where what were apparently the useless articles were thrown, earmarked for the furnace. The backside of a pair of greasy denim trousers flanked a vast rubber corset, leering with pink obscenity.

"Now, up, Piron." He was squatting on his heels. I got up shakily, both wrists pulling. He cursed, sharply. I saw that we were tethered round one of the rusty iron support pillars. My right and his left hand were tethered by regulation handcuffs. Our other two wrists were sweatily embraced by thick wire, twisted and cut off in jagged ends.

"Now do what I tell you. We've maybe got five minutes. Behind my right lapel I've got a cuff key taped. Use your teeth."

I nuzzled his suit-coat. My teeth fastened and ripped.

"Don't drop it." But I had.

He wasted no time cursing. Like two men in an involved balancing act we slid down to our knees. He bent his head and nuzzled among the year-old filth. He spat between clenched teeth, bending his neck round and bending towards the cuffs. I heard his breath wheezing down his nose. There was a sharp, metallic click. I reeled back and nearly fell, the slight pulling of the handcuffs gone.

He thrashed his free hand momentarily in the air, groped and found a handkerchief, and tried it on the wire on our other wrists. He spent perhaps a minute. When they came away his finger-tips dripped redly.

"No good, no time, we need cutters. Keep in step." The three benches yielded nothing except an ingrained stench and an assortment of knives.

"God damn it," he said, "they must have wire cutters." But not where we could see. Finally we selected a couple of knives, with five-inch blades and points.

A faint infantile memory of a three-legged race, the starlings wheeling overhead in the September air, hit me as we limped along. He placed me, back to the wall, against the hinge of an iron door.

"There are two of them." He blasphemed. "I was too astonished. Fool thing for a cop. Two tough ones, old-timers. I wasn't quite out: they went through this door. When they come in, don't mess about. Finish them as they come through. Right?"

I nodded. The seconds ticked on. I glanced and saw that the red rawness of my wrist had turned to sickly white. Gangrene would be the next stage, a few hours off, if I should live so long.

He said, "Taking their time. Marcello's a schedule boy. He'd be having a bite with a couple of impeccable witnesses, they'd phone him and he'd slip out for fifteen minutes. That's why we aren't dead. He won't risk any slip-up."

There wasn't much more to say. Perhaps it was eight minutes when we heard the key.

"Come out in step," he muttered.

I didn't consciously think of it. I've searched, but I'm sure it did not cross my mind. He'd placed me on the right. When the door swung back, therefore, I was at the edge of it, which gave me just that split second ahead as I scuttled sideways and sank the knife, swiftly upward-jabbing, into the throat below a surprised, grizzled-eyebrowed face. I continued sideways and heard Gould give a muffled curse. The other guy reacted fast and stepped backward so that Gould's forward, amateurish (I had time to register) strike to the chest merely ripped his sleeve and perhaps his forearm. I saw the glint of a gun, the explosion tore at my ear drums, as my disengaged knife swung upwards and sideways, tore into the gunman's abdomen. I twisted the knife before Gould's weight fell forward and I screamed as I gave way to the tearing of the wire biting into my flesh.

My lips were wet with blood. I had passed out for a few minutes. My feet clawed the slippery floor. I got to my knees. Gould alone was peaceful. He had fallen propped against the door. Death had washed away the lines of ribaldry and cynicism. He looked oddly boyish. The first gunman lay with surprise overlaying the deep etching of his face. The other, sharp, predatory as a rat, still pumped a little blood from severed arteries. Presently it ceased.

They were both relatively old, perhaps something over sixty. Like valuable antiques. The old-time hood came up from the raw immigrant furnaces, clawing at the boom days, savaging back at the depression. Sure, there are latter-day crucibles, but gentler ones. Social security has saved many a throat. These were the old-timers, the guys you still had to employ if you really wanted the big chill.

I peeped out. There was a flight of iron stairs, the same dim lighting. I stuck my bloody hand into the inside of the rat-faced man's coat and found a pistol. I worked the breech with my teeth. A cartridge bruised my lips. Presently footsteps came, soft and sure.

His description hadn't ever mentioned blue eyes, that I had recalled. It was probably a common slip. You read "swarthy Italian", and visualise liquid brown eyes, habit overlaying the printed word. But they were mild and blue and looked at the gun I held in my right hand, the other straining against the solid clay that was Gould. I felt his personality, deceptively persuasive until you turned your back, noted how the white hands were carefully raised to chest level. He was medium height, fattish, impeccably dressed. His voice was gentle and calm. He kept on coming, his hands perceptibly rising.

"I heard gunshots as my car was passing," his hands continued upwards above his head. He was confident.

So would his lawyer be, and his chauffeur. Mr. Marcello hears gunshots and investigates. Finds a brutal crime. I wouldn't blame the D.A. if he never went to trial. Two dead old hoods from out of town. Mr. Marcello would be tweedily surveying the jury.

I shot four times fast. The first and second, he stood balanced on the iron stair, surprise in his face. He began to fall as I fanned across his chest. There was a thud like a bag of old clothes as he bounced once and hit the ground in front of the door.

I tried to keep the gun steady and fight back nausea as I waited long minutes. Automatically I tabulated the three large sacks outside the door and wondered vaguely who the extra shroud was meant for.

No one came. I did some thinking. I rummaged horridly around the floor near the elder of the two dead men and found his gun, dropping mine into the mess on the floor. Still holding one gun I clasped Gould, feeling a horrible wetness. Pushing him rather than carrying him, I crawled out. My bloody hands pawed Marcello. No gun. I guessed he hadn't carried one for years. I wiped the gun on my shirt, pressed Marcello's fingers to it and allowed it to drop from his flaccid grasp to the floor.

One of the sacks was heaving slightly. I looked inside onto the face of the informer, Duggan. He was breathing stertorously and looked much older than I remembered. He'd been a lucky man in an unhealthy profession; I'd never heard of him even getting his nose punched up to then. Moaning from the pain from my tethered wrist, I got Gould over my shoulder. Pulling at the iron staircase with the crook of my other arm, I got erect, my feet slipping slightly from the loathsome slime on them. I rubbed them one at a time until they gripped. Half pulling myself, half walking, I tottered up the steep flight. There was a landing sixteen stairs up, the narrow street door closed and the precautionary inner bar in place. I hesitated. If Marcello's car was waiting outside—and I doubted it—I would be in trouble. I climbed again, two more flights leading onto cheerless iron landings, my breath wheezing like an asthmatic old man's.

Another flight and my knees began an involuntary trembling. There was an acrid, bitter taste in my mouth. I had reached the top of the lower portion of the building. The iron landing was bigger, covered with cases holding empty bottles. Further progress was denied by a concrete wall. At the side facing the upper street was an iron door. I tried it and found it locked. With the gun I hammered a staccato prayer, scraping my knuckles even more.

I could hear nothing through the door. My mind told me that it would never open. That I was trapped here with Gould until morning came and the dreary rummaging among old clothes commenced. Incredulously I saw the light come through as it swung back. I lurched forward, pushing past a white face that emitted strangled sounds.

It was a night club. A big room filled with the tobacco smoke and the noise of the extreme fag-end of the night. About a quarter of the tables were filled. But faces and movements were frozen, as if a collection of waxworks were posed over waxen food. At the end, a four-piece band still played and half a dozen couples slowly gyrated on the dance floor. A man with longish glossy hair hit a whining note through the mike. Slowly the band stopped, mid-chord. A note like a muffled belch came from a saxophone. I found myself surveying a stiffly starched shirtfront.

"For God's sake take him off me." I felt myself falling

forward onto a white table and saw a half-cut Roquefort cheese coming into my face. Dimly I heard the crash and the tinkle of broken crockery.

I just stayed there bent over the table, hearing noise and commotion, then a strident noise over the microphone as somebody shouted through. I still clutched Gould.

Memory is a choosy thing. Somebody I would like to have thanked afterwards organised a team of waiters to pick me up and disengage Gould from me. I found myself seated, with Gould propped on two chairs beside me. I leaned to take the pressure off my wrist and said something about wire cutters.

Presently the place crowded with cops. Every prowl car for miles must have pulled in. I recognised two detachments of the dock division. I felt a sting in my free arm and looked up and saw that somebody had put a hypo into me.

"There's a man downstairs who's injured," I told the doctor. My head cleared a little and I saw a grey-headed man with a dour expression looking down at me with a worried air. With an effort of will I remembered him as McMurdo, the homicide inspector, whose expression mirrored his personality, astute, close-mouthed, with no vices except an occasional lapse into irony.

An electronic flash flickered twice briefly, and then somebody knelt and worked on my wrist. I felt the agony of blood coming back into dying flesh and rocked.

Nobody seemed to care about that. They were watching Gould's body being carried away. A couple of uniformed men guided me out to a prowl car. At the precinct house a surgeon put stitches into my wrist, gave me a tetanus shot and said I should rest my arm for at least a week and consult a doctor if there was no improvement. It took maybe an hour before they took me in to see McMurdo. Beside him sat a senior Assistant D.A., a hard-faced old man named Ricardo.

I saw my wallet on the desk. I didn't remember anyone taking it.

"Mr. Piron," said McMurdo, "would you like to make a voluntary statement?"

I told him about the shortage in the cutlery inventory, about the call from Duggan, and the little that Gould had told me of his own capture.

To give myself a little more time, I asked for cigarettes. When I had lit one I said, "The door opened inwards. We stationed ourselves so that it would mask us momentarily as it opened. Gould was nearest the hinge. Therefore he was a trifle slower and missed with the knife. One of the men shot him just before I stabbed him. I seized a gun from his shoulder holster, looked round the door, saw Marcello coming down fast, gun in hand, and shot him four times."

"An unnecessary number of shots, the police surgeon says. You killed him first time." The Assistant D.A. looked at me distastefully.

I shrugged and there was a long silence. A sixth sense told me that McMurdo was thinking of how the useful cop was killed and the expendable private eye survived. I couldn't help thinking that it would never be quite the same with me around headquarters. Facts wither away, only resentful sentiment remains.

They took me through the story about seven ways. I stuck to my simple, basic statements. Nobody was fooled. We were a gun short, to begin with. Marcello was wearing a closely-tailored tuxedo, and nobody with any sense would expect one of the hoods to be without a weapon.

Nobody, however, cared much for Marcello's demise. Eventually I signed a nice, simple, short statement, but that wasn't all.

"Mr. Piron," said McMurdo, with hangman's suavity, "you were investigating the death of a Harry Siskin. Gould was interested in the fact. He was told yesterday morning that the department was not interested. Was, in fact, there a connection you knew of between Marcello and Siskin's death?"

"All I uncovered was that Siskin, who got a living writing for the papers, was after a story on Marcello. Gould had an obsession about Marcello." I saw McMurdo suck his upper lip: he didn't care for any aspersion to be cast on his brightest young man.

"And you may as well know that I had contacted Marcello's current girl, dame by the stage name of Merlina, and also a Mrs. Sybil Green, a former one. A couple of nights ago three of his punkier punks tried to beat me up. It's on your blotter somewhere. I think that was routine, probably Marcello didn't even know. Maybe it was a routine chore for his boys. Then somebody tipped him off at Las Vegas that some tough guy was making a play for his bed, so he flew back yesterday morning. Maybe he cared so much as to give me a nice watery grave. Those bags he used were big mail ones, as stout as a coffin and more durable. Have you identified the hoods?"

"We've had descriptions and prints on the wire for over an hour," said Ricardo.

"What happened originally, I guess, is that Duggan, who they probably threatened into phoning me, was slated for killing along with me. But Gould butted in. The old-time hoods learned how to carry out instructions to the letter. So they had a third man and a policeman to boot. Before killing us all they went back for instructions. Maybe they weren't so smart."

We went over it for a further half-hour, until the clock said four. Then a plainclothesman came in with a message. McMurdo read it aloud. The dead men had been identified fairly easily. The older one had beaten two charges of murder, the rat-faced one three. One worked the San Francisco waterfront and the other lived in Chicago. They had worked together at one time.

The tension was less. Although it had followed logically, it eased matters definitely to establish that the two were hardened oldsters, professional purveyors of the big sleep since the mid-twenties. One of Marcello's out-of-town con-tacts would have done the arranging. A nice professional job which backfired. Ricardo, the Assistant D.A., unbent so far as to offer me a cigarette from his case.

Something had been niggling at the back of my mind. Finally the thought came through.

"I want to make a phone call."

Their expressions hardened. Finally McMurdo said, "As long as it is not to a newspaper and you do it in front of us, it's okay."

"I want to telephone a man called J. R. P. Pout. All I'm going to say is that Marcello is dead."

I thought I saw a faint flicker in the eyes of the Assistant D.A. My statement plainly meant nothing to McMurdo.

I got Pout second ring, and watched the Inspector's hand ready to grab the handset if I went out of line.

Imperturbably Pout said, after a second-long pause, "I see. Thank you, Piron." Without formality he replaced his receiver.

"May I ask what that was about?" asked McMurdo. His voice was on edge, owing to Gould's death. I was sorry.

I shrugged and told him maybe nothing.

That didn't satisfy him, but Ricardo baulked the angry words. "I think that we'll let the matter rest." McMurdo's mouth set in a stubborn line.

We fiddled around some more and McMurdo was gathering up my wallet to return it to me as a signal that we were through when his telephone rang. I could see from his face that he'd given no incoming calls as an instruction.

"Who? What? I'm sorry, sir, I didn't expect *you* to ring."

He listened for maybe four minutes with as near animation as it was possible for his dour face to express. "I quite understand, sir." He rang off and expressed a blasphemy quite out of character.

"Don't go away, Piron. Just stand outside the door a few minutes."

When he let me in, he wore the gloomy expression of a man who is on a hot seat and knows it. Ricardo, veteran of a couple of hundred court battles, smoked impassively. We sat there until the door opened and J. R. P. Pout thrust his personality into the room and made the battered furniture look even seedier.

As he shook hands, adding that he thought he had some slight acquaintance with Mr. Ricardo, I saw that his ruddy jowls were close-shaved. He couldn't have found time; then I remembered that his car would be chauffeured and have a point for an electric razor. He wore a soberly-coloured casual outfit which he made look like a million dollars. I looked at him and despaired. He sat down and glanced through my statement.

"A pity about the plainclothesman! A good one?"

"About my best," said McMurdo.

"I'm sorry," he said shortly, but in such a way that it made the tough old headquarters cop look better.

"Now," said Pout. "I know, Inspector, that my inter-vention—hell, interference—is irksome."

McMurdo made a friendly gesture, as if King William had asked a game-keeper if he resented the seduction of his daughter.

"Well," said Pout, "co-operation's particularly pleasant. But I'll be in your hair only to the extent that it is my duty to go over Marcello's personal possessions first and take away what I may consider fit."

That was fine with McMurdo.

A civilian clerk brought in the contents of Marcello's clothes, a thick wallet, a key ring, a couple of handkerchiefs, some small change, a combination cigarette case and lighter, and a leather belt with three more keys firmly stapled to it.

"Interesting," said Pout. "The annotation says he wore this round his waist." With quick methodical gestures he stacked them in a heavy briefcase. "I'll go through these later. Right now I want to lose no time in going over Marcello's apartment. He gave me a quick glance. "I know you've had a bad time, Piron, but I'd appreciate it if you'd come along. I'd like a quarter of an hour's chat before the night's out."

He conferred briefly and authoritatively with McMurdo and we waited ten minutes before a photographer and three other guys came in—a narcotics squad detail thoroughly trained in the art of searching premises. Three police cars took us out. I thought there was sullen fear on the face of the liftman who took us up, but I couldn't be sure. I didn't enter immediately. Perhaps the effect of the shot I was given in the restaurant had worn off, but I leaned against the wall of the hallway and dry-retched, conscious of the stink of violent death on my stained clothes.

I watched them ring the bell and wait. Then a stocky plainclothesman pounded with a pair of mahogany-looking fists. Finally they used a key on Marcello's pocket ring. I leaned against the wall, waiting for the nausea to clear. Uncomprehendingly I watched the stocky detective tear out again and sprint for the lift. My body felt heavy and sacklike and I allowed it to slide down the wall, feeling the merciful relief of thick carpet. I cupped my head in my hands. Presently the detective returned, with four uniformed men and a little man with a doctor's bag. They ran past me.

Eventually I felt well enough to climb cautiously erect. I tottered through into the apartment. In the big living area I remembered so well was the glare of the photographer's lights. As I came through, my foot slithered on something. I looked down and saw a pile of little red fish and saw that the heavy carpet was saturated with water. The plate glass fish tanks that partitioned the room had been battered and mostly smashed. Great shards of the heavy glass glinted on the carpet. Already the little, flaming bodies were fading to a dull, deathly white.

I saw her on the ground not far from the record player we had used. Her face was deeply buried in the carpet. Her fair hair was matted with blood and something else. The house coat she had worn had slid up and I gazed at the trim, resilient thighs that I remembered. A yard away the merciless light reflected on metal, a short steel bar.

No feeling, mental or physical, bothered me. I was too drained. I blundered away to a small armchair and sat on it, masking my eyes with one hand against the light. The sounds of death seeped through the murmur of the doctor's voice, the sounds of feet walking out in unison. When I opened my eyes, she had gone. I thought I detected the faint smell of perfume in the air.

Pout was standing like a man who sees time slipping away and can do nothing. Ricardo and McMurdo had their heads close together.

Finally I heard Ricardo say, with unaccustomed emotion, "The bastard! I saw her dance one night. Vital little thing."

McMurdo glanced at me, cop-shrewd. "How well did you know her?"

I wiped the sweat from my forehead with one palm. I couldn't guess how I looked. "Sunday night. I wanted her to identify Harry Siskin. She admitted seeing him a couple of times. Long and short of it, I spent the night here. That's all. I didn't get in touch with her again. First reason time, second reason how I figured her."

I heard my weak, old-man voice die away.

"I think we'll have the doctor back to look at Piron," said Pout. I felt grateful to him.

"Sure. Murphy, get that doctor back pronto! Sorry, Piron, but how did you figure her?"

"She was a warm generous girl. She lived with a hood like Marcello and had him wrapped up. So she had an occasional one-night frolic with a stranger, just very occasionally when she felt like it. I thought that it all ended in the morning, no repeat performances. It tormented Marcello, but he wanted her too much to kick her out. Maybe she went too far. I dunno."

McMurdo thought for a while before adding, "Marcello could have had you slated for the big one. Maybe he told her and she got mad. He went berserk and used that bar on her. It fits."

It fitted. I folded back into my chair while the search party got to work. They were good and methodical. First they stripped up the carpet in sections, moving the furniture steadily back. I stuck around until they started on the upholstery and then found another room which looked like a small dining-room. I waited there until the doctor came. He grunted at the hand, fetched out the inevitable needle, and then immobilised it in a plaster splint. He gave me a sling and told me that was all he could do until the morning.

I went to the bedroom with its outsize bed. Pout was there. He worked easily, methodically, tidily, rather different from the men outside. It was obvious that he was used to the kind of search that leaves no trace. The others just went bull-headed after something.

I went to one of the wardrobes and found filmy gowns. The other had men's stuff in it. I took down the longest dressing-gown I could see.

"Would you clear this?"

His eyes, absorbed in scanning a drawer, glanced up briefly. With him you did not have to labour explanations.

"Good idea." He spread the gown, an ornate brocade, on the floor, scanned it carefully, ran his fingers down the seams, reversed it and repeated the process. "Clear," he said, and tossed it to me.

The bathroom as I remembered it was about half the size of my apartment. In the event memory had exaggerated, it was not perhaps more than a third. Marcello had adapted the "his" and "hers" principle to the extent of having two sunken tiled baths, one azure blue, the other a delicate shade of rose. I studied the various bottles and tubes above each and decided hers had been the pink one. The water flowed in through a cunning tap fashioned in the form of a Cupid's face. A device regulated the exact temperature. I adjusted it, located the bath essence and sank down into a hazy cloud of the perfume I remembered so well. After nearly an hour, I climbed out and used two bath towels which felt three inches thick. I scrubbed with them until my flesh felt red and then donned the dressing-gown. I looked distastefully at the wreckage of my clothing in its sordid heap upon the tessellated flooring. I had to wear my shoes, discarding the socks. The black leather had an unpleasant brown patina and the laces were stiff to touch. After I had put them on I washed my hands. I flinched from the face in the mirror.

My wristwatch told me that it was six thirty. I went to the bedroom and, ignoring Pout, sprawled on the bed and was asleep in a few seconds. Not until ten to nine did he shake me gently. My muscles felt stiff and I could hardly bend, but my thoughts came clearly and crisply.

"If you don't mind, Piron." He glanced round. "Only the bed's left here and I can't see Marcello hiding things under the mattress."

He led me over to a door I had barely noticed. There were two locks, I noted on close inspection. He took out of his pocket the belt Marcello had worn underneath his clothes. Its original colour had been extinguished by grease. The two keys on it fitted the locks. He led me into a room with a plain table and chair. The room was about ten feet by twelve, and there were no windows. My eyes focused on the heavy door of the safe at the end.

He gestured. "Not a single damned thing so far and we've torn the place to bits practically. Anything would be in there. We're waiting until we can get somebody from the company who made it." He blinked at it out of bloodshot eyes. "It's the heaviest safe I've ever seen and I've had experience."

His tones were annoyed, but his glance at me was tolerantly humorous. "Now, Piron, I'd like you to run over every single goddamned thing that happened to you yesterday after you got out of bed. If you went to the john, I want to hear it."

I closed my eyes and tried a total recall. It took maybe half an hour. When I opened them I saw that his big, rather clumsy-looking hand had been inscribing very neat shorthand into a notebook.

He put the pencil neatly beside the book, and massaged his eyes.

"Thanks for a lot of things, including tipping me off about Marcello's death. Time is what we're getting very short of. I never considered Sybil Green as she quit Marcello's bed long before he got involved in the espionage angle. That was what I told you about—Siskin's tendency to go beyond his brief.

"I think that Sybil in her cups would talk to Harry about Marcello. One morning she gets remorse and tells Marcello that a guy has been getting nosey. He takes a look and finds it's the same guy who was sneaking up around Merlina. So, somehow, he stages the suicide."

He gave a sudden boyish smile. "I'm glad for you personally, Piron—not mentioning a lady's name and all that."

I had started to return the grin when the door opened. McMurdo, Ricardo and a gloomy-looking little man in clothes that gave an impression of stiffness came in. McMurdo looked as though he'd had a few hours' sleep and the Assistant D.A. had even found himself a shave.

The little man was head foreman for the safe company. His voice bore traces of the aspirate trouble common to the London Cockney, which was unfortunate as his name was Higsby.

He prodded the great steel door as if suspecting it had turned to jelly and sighed gustily through his nose.

"How long will it take to open this?"

"Without the combination?"

McMurdo restrained his impatience. "We haven't got it. His lawyers haven't got it. Period."

The man took the two keys McMurdo extended and went to the safe. "You turn one key," he said gloomily, "then insert the other and turn that. You can't turn the second until the first has turned." We heard a click. He pulled the steel knob on the door, shrugged and took the keys out. "Just a chance that they forgot the combination. We always try first, though I've never heard of it working."

I gave a faint grin at McMurdo's expression. I knew the type. Higsby would relish the weight on his shoulders, always seeking to add to it, always complaining. He would see to it that he was grossly overworked at the factory. Doubtless related Higsbys down to great-cousins "put upon him", as he would phrase it. And Higsby loved every moment of it.

"How long?"

"Tamper with the combination—it's a seven-letter one, specially ordered by the client—and two bars drop into sockets inside. You're worse off than you was before. 'Ard steel, if there's any 'arder we never 'eard of it."

He sucked a tooth and looked gloomily at the carpet.

"Look, sir, you can only do it by torch. It'd take maybe two days and three trucks of cylinders. It was built in when they put the building up."

"Two days!"

I had taken up Pout's notebook and pencil and did a calculation. I went and peered at the safe. Although you could only see the finely milled steel surface, you seemed to sense the power to resist underneath.

"With the traffic," Higsby was saying, "it might be longer even if you was to work two-shift."

I listened to them over my shoulder. Higsby preferred to remove the safe, an operation involving demolition of the wall and a crane being placed on the roof, and take it to the factory. He thought it might be a bit easier through the back of the safe.

"No short cut?" Pout kept his head.

"You can open *any* safe, sir," said Higsby doggedly. "All we can do is to make the process take too long for a burglar to try. The client specified at least fifty hours, and we always give a margin."

I fiddled with the combination and dialled seven times. As I put a little weight on the knob, the huge door, so delicately hung, slid back and opened.

Higsby saw it first. His jaw dropped. "Mr. Higsby," I said quickly, "you only have to emery-paper your finger-tips and feel the click of the tumblers."

Incredulous doubt came into his dazed fishy eyes. Pout reacted first.

"Thanks, Mr. Higsby, for your co-operation." Smoothly he guided the little man out.

The thick silence prevailed until he shut the door. He looked at me as if he had never seen me before. McMurdo didn't register such a feeling. He balanced on the balls of his feet, hard fists knotted and face shoved towards mine. He snarled deep from his taut belly: "I looked at your record, Piron. You're tough. You'll find I'm tougher."

"Better give him a chance to explain," said Ricardo, quickly.

"The combination was 2976918," I said quickly. "When you have these excessively long combinations you choose a word and translate the letters into their arithmetical place in the alphabet."

Ricardo got it first. "That makes it b..i..g..f..i..s..h".

"Sure. In his own circle Marcello liked being called the Big Fish. Kind of joke. His old man is supposed to have been a fish pedlar. Only his closest friends, mind you. If you were a punk or an enemy, you'd get your teeth bashed in. So," I finished, "I tried it."

McMurdo had the baffled look that a disgruntled child gives a conjurer. He was searching for an angle and couldn't find one.

"Thank God for you," Ricardo said. "I was thinking of having to lower that safe with the reporters and TV cameras. It's bad enough now."

"You've made a release?"

"Had to." He seemed friendly. "God, Piron, do you know what a stir you made around that restaurant? Three people were taken away with shock."

Pout, standing to the side, had swung the safe door right back. He tried each of the interior compartments. Evidently Marcello had reasoned that if the safe could be opened, further precaution was useless.

"Did you never get a search warrant here?" Ricardo asked McMurdo.

The Inspector nearly sneered. "He didn't live here. His official address, voting registration, is at a hotel two blocks away. Officially this place and everything in it belong to an attorney he employed. How could I get a warrant?"

"Shall we proceed?" asked Pout.

"I don't think we need you, Piron," snapped McMurdo.

I shrugged. "Maybe the press boys will give me a drink."
And so I stayed.

First, two policemen brought in two large steel boxes and
placed them on the floor. Pout took off his coat and Ricardo
and McMurdo stood at his side. I had to peer over their
shoulders.

The first compartment yielded a box of what looked like
pebbles. Pout whistled. "Uncut diamonds."

He hesitated, then said to McMurdo, "Put them in your
box. I'll want an expert opinion on place of origin later."

The next compartment contained jewellery, a flashing
heap of tethered fireflies as they were scooped out on to
Pout's broad palm. He said, "Also in your box and an
expert report on origin and setting."

In all there were four compartments of stones. At one
lot the Inspector sucked his breath. "I think I recognise
these, Mr. Pout, though it's not my province. A robbery
down Miami way."

Three other compartments contained notes. I estimated
around three hundred thousand, plus a big stack of Swiss
francs and some South American currency. The rest were
papers, neatly bound into folders or encased in deed boxes.

Pout flipped through them. "I'll take the paper stuff,"
he said. "Well," he added, reading rapidly at random, "he
was a methodical guy. I suppose he thought only his death
would result in the safe being opened, and then he wouldn't
care. You'll have quite a few guys in court from this stuff,
Inspector."

The hunting light flickered in McMurdo's eyes. The
Assistant D.A. plainly quivered like a hound. I remembered
that Ricardo had never fulfilled his wife's political ambitions.
A series of sensational, successful trials, and maybe Father
Christmas would call with a bag of nominations.

"I'll process them as soon as possible," said Pout, yawning
and looking dead on his feet. He looked at me, standing and
feeling out of it.

"McMurdo," he suggested, "about our friend Piron. Just
as a suggestion, what about putting him into a hospital

police ward for a few days? You see, Piron, you'll be pestered by reporters otherwise and you look all in."

I nodded. The other possibility, which he didn't mention, was that McMurdo might slap me into a cell as a material witness. I preferred hospital. It seemed attractive right then.

McMurdo hadn't been able to do anything much with the front of the building. We glanced out of the living-room windows and saw the patient gum-chewing crowd. The sun glinted on optical lenses. But he had cordoned off the back delivery area and the luggage lift. We walked to the door. The little fish were turning black and had started to smell high. I flapped after them in my dressing-gown and crouched down in the back of a police car. The police ward had a private entrance with its own lift. Unmolested I followed an orderly into a small but private room, got between the rough sheets and closed my eyes. I awakened in the late afternoon.

Another orderly peeped in and returned with a tray with bacon and eggs and coffee on it. He looked at me quizzically and put a bunch of afternoon papers on the side cabinet. First I ate, then I looked at the papers.

Merlina got the number one spot. A girl in her job has dozens of professional photographs taken, and had they plastered them! The mannered, postured body seemed remote from the one I knew. My photograph (see page three) was horrible. I cast back in my memory and alighted upon a christening party. Half plastered, I had gazed at the squalling infant and tried a benign smile. Usually I avoid photographs, but this was a social occasion, an old friend's filling quiver—I remembered he was in the newsprint business. My eyes seemed faintly crossed and my face strangely lop-sided. My lips were parted over my teeth. They had all used copies of this print and one of the happier caption writers commented on the "habitual, wolf-like, bare-teethed snarl which . . .".

The spokesman for the D.A. had been cagey, so most of the story was colour stuff. The Marcello angle lacked facts —nobody knew enough. When they came to me, towards the end of most stories, after the lead in one or two, I emerged as the tough, relentless, killing detective popularised by TV. One sheet described me as "in World War II the crack, remorseless killer for Military Intelligence", which rankled. Hand on heart, the only guy I even nearly killed in World War II was an Australian lieutenant. In Cairo. He had stolen my little French girl. Additionally he had made away with two bottles of Scotch, which did hurt. At that he half killed me as much as I half killed him when we met up.

The Agency's name was mentioned over and over. Sometimes the Old Man said any publicity was good publicity, and other times he grew shy and reversed that judgment. I reached out and put a call through to the office. The switchboard for this section of the hospital had somebody who sounded like a cop on it.

The Old Man's voice boomed richly along the wire. "Good to hear you, Piron. I decided to let you make touch in your own time. Are they holding you? I'll get . . ."

"No," I said. "I'm in the police ward with the semi-lunatics, all male unfortunately. I guess I'd like to stay a couple of days, maybe. I got lumps."

"Nothing bad?"

"Nothing." I wondered why he was so cheerful.

"When I read those papers I had recourse to the private bottle. Then, do you know what, the calls started to pour in. At least eight new accounts. Of course they all ask for Mr. Piron personally. Let's see, 'oddly magnetic, impelling eyes, ice cold, that impale the witness'."

"For God's sake who said that?"

"An out-of-town sheet. An old friend of yours from L.A. spent his own money telephoning it in."

I guessed who the bastard was.

"And women," he said, vice leering, the old goat. "Little notes on sweet-smelling paper by special delivery. Dames phoning in and blocking the lines up. A couple of telegrams. Listen to this. 'Darling Killer. I await you at room 222, Hotel Imperial, at midnight.'"

As I listened to his horse laugh I thought of the queerness of it. I have seen a murderer, the rap narrowly beaten, push his way through the women on the court-room steps, seen the little notes pushed into his hands.

"No sign of a darling five foot seven, well stacked, green eyes, hair the colour of old copper?"

"No, Piron." One thing I like about him is that he knows when to joke and when not to.

"If she calls or writes, give her this number."

"Say," he said, "I'll write a note, just to let her know where you are, and send it round."

"That would be good. Just one thing else. My spare key is in the safe. If you could get one of the help to send round a case of clothes I'd be glad."

I wished him well, threw the papers on the floor, and lay there watching the ceiling, ears waiting for the telephone to ring.

It didn't.

I remembered Duggan, and the orderly told me that he was in a private room. There was also a squat plainclothesman on a chair inside the door. He made no move to stop me as I flapped along in a drab towelling dressing-gown. Duggan was conscious, flat on the hard mattress. I noticed he had aged twenty years. As he saw me he put one hand under the bedclothes and produced his dentures, which took maybe ten of them off. He stared at me with the honest eyes that most petty crooks seem to have.

"I'm sorry, Mr. Piron," he said.

I gave him a shrug and asked how he was.

"They thought the head was fractured at first, but it was just a bad concussion. Honest, Mr. Piron, I wouldn't have fingered you for a thousand bucks! But they told me what they were going to do if I didn't play." His face went greyer as he remembered and he swallowed hard. I could imagine the things that two competent professional hoods could think up to do with a man like Duggan.

"When did they pick you up?"

"Around six. I was hanging around a bar looking for a

fellow I had business with when they came in. They just sat one on each side. One of them said they'd like a word with me. By that time I'd got them spotted—real old-timers and good at it. So I went out and got into their car, a three-year-old Chevvy, and sat in the back with one of them. The other drove."

"They talk?"

He shook his head and winced. "Those guys don't talk on a job. They drove around very carefully. They'd park for twenty minutes and turn on the radio; then drive off again. Three times one of them got out of the car. I guessed it was to phone. It happened at seven thirty, then at nine, and finally just after ten. After that they drove to somewhere near a suburban station and parked. It's the safest place, nobody bothers about you."

I gave him a cigarette. From the corner of my eye I saw that the cop was looking bored. I might just as well have got Duggan's story from the police record, but it passed the time.

"Then one of them talked to me, the one with the scar on his lip. Like I said they told me what they could do to me." His breathing became slow and deep, like a distance runner.

"Then they said they knew you'd talked to me earlier in the day and what was it about? I told them. They told me I was to phone you and say exactly what I did. I had to go over it six times. Around midnight they pulled up outside a call box and one of them stood behind me while I called you."

"Where was the box?"

His faint voice grew edgy. "For God's sake, I was near to fainting, Piron. I kept telling myself that I'd never get out alive."

"Then?"

"He walked me back to the car and opened the door. I remember starting to get in and that's all. Next thing I woke up here."

"Okay, Duggan," I said. "No hard feelings, I guess." I

dropped the cigarettes on the coverlet and went back.

In the evening, when my nostrils had become accustomed to the whiffs which crept under the closed door of my private clinical cell, I received two callers. J. R. P. Pout was as ever immaculate. I thought he must have some kind of foam rubber inside that puffed him out in spite of lack of sleep. With him was the Assistant D.A., Ricardo. With him only the scent of success kept the weary flesh alert. There were fleshy bags around his blasé, clever, grey eyes.

"You're a hero, boy," beamed Pout. "So say the newspapers."

I liked him with my eyes. "So say the ladies by private messenger, friend." Ricardo gave me a professional paw. It felt like an old rug.

An awkward silence, one of those which start with a misplaced second and lag into a lifetime unless somebody coughs, hovered around, but Pout said rapidly:

"Just a strategy-planning call, old lad, with maybe a tactic or two on the agenda. I thought Ricardo and I could pester you simultaneously."

I had been grinning helpfully long enough to reassure Ricardo. He had a lot to win or lose. He gave a courtroom cough and a steady look.

"Mr. Pout told me that he thought you wouldn't be unduly interested in what we might call his side of this business, eh, Piron?"

"Hell," I said. "Who's Pout? As far as I know, he's my fish supplier."

It was wrong, not quite the note. Ricardo pursed his lips and Pout coloured a little.

"I mean," I said contritely, "I practically never heard of him. If you say so, I never heard of either of you."

This time I got Ricardo's political grin. Warm it was, calculated to warm the cockles of any voter way back to Douglas Social Credit.

"Right," said Ricardo. "I felt that you'd co-operate that way. Nevertheless, we thought you deserved to be filled in on events."

Pout added, annoyance in his voice: "And there's a Grand Jury, nosey as ever, in session, plus the fact that you can't go around shooting people without a Coroner."

Ricardo's professional eyebrow was hoisted. He settled for a Harvard smile. "We'd better get it on the table. Mr. Pout's side is out, okay?"

I nodded.

"Right. He's done a great job looking through the stuff we got out of that safe. It comes out like this. Marcello kept a written record, plus receipts, plus photostats, of what he had. There's a lot of stuff about his early rackets. Then he used Sybil Green's money to go big-time and subsequently semi-legitimate.

"A lot of his business was money conversion. If you were a racketeer with a lot of hot money, Marcello would convert it for you into a legitimate business investment. The process was ingenious, via holding companies and capital gains. For a million bucks you got back maybe half in solid, accountancy-proofed cash.

"Sometimes they weren't in the racket. You might be a business man with a hot wad of notes you were scared of keeping until you heard about Marcello. So you saw him and got it converted to white money—except he had the records so that he could always ask you a favour.

"Third were the embezzlers, the really hot boys that got out to, say, France, where you can't get extradited if you've got the money to fee the lawyers. Before you went you gave the loot to Marcello. He gave you thirty per cent, and didn't cheat. The same applied to hot jewellery."

"So you'll be busy prosecuting for the next year," I said.

The angle was clear. Ricardo had snatched firm hold of the evidence, all set to be the best fighting, gang-busting attorney in history. Pout's connection would back him, for favours returned. It suited me.

"A fair bag, eh, Ricardo?" said Pout.

The attorney twisted his wide mouth and rubbed his hand through his hair.

"I'll make it clear, Piron. First, there are the 'legitimate' tax evaders. They'll be turned over to the income-tax assessors. They'll receive a demand that will shake them to the marrow bones, but they'll pay rather than face criminal proceedings. That way, we make an example and Uncle S. gets his profit. Of the racketeers in the same position, some we just assess, and some we send to gaol. But that's all Federal. What I've got is evidence to prosecute in four unsolved murder cases, solutions to perhaps eight armed robberies, and enough to bring a couple of embezzlers back from overseas."

"That still leaves the inquest," I said, feeling surly.

"Tomorrow at nine," he said. "It'll catch the afternoon papers that way. Just run through your police statements— I'll have a look over them with you before the hearing—and it's justifiable homicide. It should not last an hour."

"And the Grand Jury?"

"Unless they are using the powers of this antique apparatus to their own advantage, D.A.s are chary of this institution, a hang-over from a robuster age."

He shuffled. "I wouldn't disguise from you that the Foreman is trying. He's not a man to be discounted."

"So?"

He put his palms upwards. "Tomorrow is Saturday. I'd like to stall them so that I can have the week-end in which to issue warrants."

Pout had gathered up his pigskin gloves. He patted me on the shoulder. "Thanks for the lot, Jim. I guess I'm not necessary here. So long Ricardo."

I watched him go and wearily lay back in bed while Ricardo told me about the Grand Jury. I listened with half an ear. Even with their theoretical powers, Grand Juries can't do much if you have the District Attorney by your side.

The room was heavy with the smoke from his cigar. I suddenly thought of Sybil Green, Marcello's willy-nilly partner, and suggested that she might be difficult to control.

He gave a heavy gesture, the political gesture which public officials give when Great Affairs of State necessitate a little compromise with abstract values. He was not quite comfortable.

"We haven't anything against her, at least nothing we could get without her co-operation," he said ponderously. "She fell for Marcello. He used her money to get going in the Big Time. Nevertheless she was smart enough to keep sufficient records on him to give some assurance against being killed. Pout and I had a word with her four hours ago. She turned her records over to us, and she'll catch a night flight to Europe."

"Did she know much?"

"Most of it is too out of date to have practical value, but she had a couple of killings on him, stuff he organised fifteen years ago. They were two men who wouldn't sell him a gambling concession. Additionally she had some figures on income-tax evasion. Her attorneys have handled the financial side with Marcello since they split up."

If I'd wanted to get rid of him, it was the right way. He gave me a double-handed clasp and was through the door.

After he had gone I lay awake listening for the silent telephone to ring. Presently the orderly, a cross-eyed man with a post-mortem look about him, offered me supper. I refused and asked for his best brand of sleeping pill, good for six hours. After a while he came back with two capsules. I took them and passed out.

The mirror next morning wasn't too unkind. A lot of the bruising had gone, bits of sticking plaster looked vaguely romantic. My wrist still hurt after a couple of shots from the doctor and felt as if it was straining to get through the bandage.

Ricardo proved right about the inquest. John Christopher Marcello did wilfully murder Gwenda Stein, alias Merlina. Edward Roosevelt Flower wilfully murdered Edward Gould with Hyam Blasnovitch an accessory before and after. I, James Piron, in fear of my life, justifiably killed the said Flower, the said Blasnovitch and the said Marcello. Amen. A city's duty done. At the inquest Ricardo, confidence oozing, put the horses round the ring, but the Grand Jury was a little different.

The Foreman had a bad impediment in his speech but he was a wholesale butcher, a trade in which you are either good or gone, depending on your knowledge of human nature. The Assistant D.A. wasn't very happy about him. I think we could have had trouble. For one thing he had enough knowledge of slaughter-houses to figure out that our story regarding the cellar didn't come out very well. Owing to his impediment and the fact that his occupation didn't suit him for a diplomatic role, his jury trod all over him, including a couple of guys who were interested in Organised Vice. Did I think that the Marcello fortune came out of whore-houses? I caught the D.A.'s eye and opined that undoubtedly the agents of Satan made a pile out of laying such traps for our young manhood. Actually the big dough isn't there any longer, what with overheads and the fact that the girls must eat and dress, unless it's a part of some larger racket, such as plushy gambling. I fumbled about in the memory banks and located some hot magazine articles about vice in high places. They leaped upon my words like hounds on a spoor. The Foreman chewed his harelip and measured me with his eyes for carcass weight, but he might as well have tried to stop an avalanche. Had I known Miss Merlina? I had. Watching their tongues flicker over dry lips I gave my second spiel, the Harems of the Damned, the houris who whored with gangsters. I thought vaguely that I should get a transcript and send it Hollywood way. It filled the morning and a little of the afternoon until, exhausted by vicarious sin, the Jury accepted Ricardo's suggestion of adjournment for the week-end.

The Assistant D.A. remarked from the comfortable depths of the official car: "By Monday we'll have warrants out and they'll be *sub judice*. I'll throw the Foreman some nice juicy bone he can't resist. The warrants will get the Press off our backs. The Grand Jury will be happy and then I can get to work."

He was happy. I was a good boy. The smell of the Green

Upman poking from his thin lips mingled with the sweet anticipation of success. His wife—I remembered that she looked like a very small and determined pony, a trifle gone at the legs—would love him, and that and heaven would make his reward.

"Perhaps you would be good enough to drop me back at my apartment. The heat should have died sufficiently . . ."

But he didn't love me enough. The odd, political shiftiness flickered through his eyes. He guessed another night wouldn't hurt. After all it was really a matter for Inspector McMurdo.

I knew when I was beaten. Deftly, almost casually, he refused my offers to drop me nearby and watched, waving genially, until I was inside the door.

The Office had sent me round two mailbags of letters and telegrams with a sarcastic note attached that was supposed to make me feel good. It passed the rest of the day. The number that were plain abusive startled me, mostly on "living by the sword" lines. I wished they had been in that stinking cellar instead of me. The plain congratulatory ones, the invitations to address Junior Chambers of Commerce, followed them to the floor. It left me with a tidy pile of maybe two hundred "love" letters, and a dozen of the threatening variety. I took the latter first. All of them purported to come from friends of the departed and the least imaginative proposed a slow process of evisceration. Oddly, you don't get too many threats in my business. They don't kill or maim when there is no percentage. What's over is over as far as the professional crims are concerned. Most of the nose-punching directed at me has come from the male (and one female) co-respondents trapped by my peerings over transom windows and through the keyholes of bedroom closets. I have had cause to examine hundreds of letters written by crooks. Nowadays most of them are literate. Hell, you can't spend around six thousand dollars educating a kid, any kid, plus providing elaborate prison libraries and educational projects, without instilling something! And these days the formsheet writers are so fancy that the guys who hang around the poolrooms are getting quite a vocabulary. Ten of the thirteen were written in dialogue straight out of *Black Mask*, 1926 edition, college kids tugging at my leg. I tossed them on the floor. The remaining four were nicely and anonymously typed on old machines, not too fancifully phrased. I stuck the envelopes and letters together and put them aside for McMurdo and his cohorts to take a look at, just in case.

That left me with two hundred invitations to dally. The second scrutiny made it one hundred and thirty-seven because the difference came from guys named Roderic who wanted to talk to me earnestly about psychology. I settled down to my reading. The cross-eyed orderly who had come in to complain about the mess I was making on the floor squatted near my feet and sucked his teeth while he acted as second reader. It was very cosy. Methodically I pinned the photographs to the letters and shuffled them into what looked like order of seniority. In the interest of morality I placed the top and bottom thirds aside in a cardboard box. The orderly and I conducted a two-man discussion and like French politicians formed two parties. He violently endorsed the claims of a red-haired young lady who did ballet-dancing underwater at fairs. I pointed out that such carryings on inevitably result in muscular development at places I feel no muscles should be. I supposed that working in a police ward distorted one's taste. For myself I ogled a number photographed on a bearskin rug which looked very cosy considering the weather. It was in colour and she was a natural blonde. She signed that she was a countess and gave a prosperous apartment house address and her telephone number.

"What's the use?" asked my gloomy friend as he began to sweep up the discarded paper.

"The use, friend?"

"All written by school kids, I'll bet."

"I went to a tough school, pal, and none of us could write like that."

"You'd be surprised," he said. "Anyway, then there's

the jokers. Take that countess, now. You go down there, grab her when she opens the door, and you'll find you've got an old lady of eighty-nine and that the janitor wrote the note because she reported him."

"Then that janitor sure has a nice-looking wife! We'll see." I gave the switchboard the number and waited. Her voice was thick and sweet like navy rum, with the same bitter, intriguing undertone to it.

"I'm Jim Piron. Did you send me a note?"

"Yes." That was all. No elaboration. Just soft breathing coming over the line.

"It was succinct and all that."

"Yes." She seemed to be a yes-girl all right. Her talent seemed literary.

"Thank you for your good wishes, Countess. I just wished to make sure it wasn't a joke."

I put the hand-set back. The orderly finished putting the waste-paper in a sack and gave me a parting look. "I'll tell the dietician to put you on high-protein meals," was all he said.

I put her letter into my wallet and the others into the cardboard box. For my old age. When the bleak wind whistles round that little lodge in Oregon I have made six payments on, Ancient Piron will huddle his old bones before the roaring logs. "Grandson, fetch me that old cardboard box in the attic. Grandpa wants to muse."

The orderly was as good as his word. Dinner consisted of as juicy a steak as I've had, garnished Australian-wise with eggs. I felt surprised when I ate it and felt my hand going out to switch on the transistor radio that the office had packed with my things. Goodwill flowed through my veins as I finished the apple-pie.

The orderly shuffled to collect the tray and gave me his swivelling glance. "There's a lady to see you," he said. "Been hanging around an hour until permission came through."

I thought of burnished hair and comfort, sniffed the smell of lye, percolating from the corridors, heard the occasional snore from the general ward and other not so pleasant sounds, assessed the greasy blankets, checked what I knew of the value of novelty, and sighed.

"Show her in."

Somehow he looked disgruntled and sucked his teeth. "I told you," he said mysteriously.

I had the word "Gretyl" on my palate. I tensed, ready to leap out of bed, the wounded knight back from his travail, the battered warrior seeking solace in the lady's kiss.

What came in the door was her aunt.

I checked the leap but the name came out, in a kind of croak. She gave me her wise, blank, tortoise-head look.

"I'm sorry, Piron," she said. "That's why I came round. Didn't seem right, somehow, thinkin' of you just laying in here. It took me hours getting permission."

I fumbled and lit a cigarette.

"It's no good, Piron," she said. "She had her telephone unhooked all yesterday. Today she moved to another apartment, didn't want to come in with me."

"Why, for God's sake?"

"I'll take one of those cigarettes if I may," her slate eyes looked kind. "Back home, one time, we knew a kid that was in the State police. He got himself engaged to the schoolmarm. My, she was one for action—we had a few bank robbers and the like then. She was always talking about the old-time vigilantes. One day he was outside a bank when it was held up. He got a slug in his belly, but killed a couple of the bandits. The others piled into a car and eventually drove a couple of hundred feet down off a road they didn't know had had a wash-out.

"He gets out of hospital, the Governor gives him a police medal. Then, there's a plate dinner and a public subscription. Today's he's Chief, married to a nice girl who ran a diner."

"And his girl, the school teacher?"

"She doesn't like the sight of blood. She's married, with grandchildren now. She and her husband are on the parole board. They're both very tough about it all."

"So?"

She got off the truckle chair and twitched back her glasses. "So it's no good. Sorry."

I shook her hand and watched her go. Afterwards I raised hell until they gave me another capsule.

It was a grey morning next day when I attended by permission the Inspector's funeral that they gave Gould. The Mayor was there; there was a representative of the Governor; and a lot of very grim-faced cops. The Press, particularly the photographers, were noticeably obedient. A priest said what a good man had been lost in the constant warfare between Good and Bad. I sat on a hard pew and remembered his twisted grin and wondered if I would have liked him if we had really known each other. It was dull and clouded when they brought him to the graveside. The widow was there, a thin blonde upon whom prettiness still sat precariously, like the last blossom on a tree.

I managed to get McMurdo to one side after it was all over. He shuffled a bit, on the world-wide bureaucratic principle that once you're inside you should remain there, but finally relented and said he'd make the necessary arrangements for me to leave hospital.

I got my wrist dressed and hung around the ward until permission came through. I said goodbye to the cross-eyed orderly after he had lugged my suitcase to the taxi.

The apartment had been cleaned but smelled stale. I opened the back door to let in clean air and dunked the suitcase in the closet. For something to do, a nervous gesture like lighting a cigarette, I rang the office and after six tries got through. Business seemed booming, but the Old Man, falsely genial, steam-rollered any suggestion about my coming in before a week's rest.

I found my feet up on the recently cleaned couch. Cynically I guessed that they wanted me out of the way while the new clients were given the treatment. It's one thing to have the great Piron available, and quite another, anti-climactic thing to produce a beat-up, middle-aged Irishman with a two-day stubble over his bruised face.

I watched the dirty little fleecy clouds floating over equally dirty roofs and found myself suddenly sitting up and staring at the telephone. It was a feeling I knew, an atavistic pop-up from the days when my tribal ancestors were hiding in the long grass watching for Romans. My neck prickled. There were Romans around. I've learned to trust my instinct without comment.

My first whisky for three days tasted like brackish water which fundamentally it is. I tried another. It went down better. I chose four numbers from my private book and started dialling.

Two of the men I was calling were out. The other two needed time. So it was about four in the afternoon before I had finished. In the meantime I ate tinned beans and made a bad job of shaving.

When I put the receiver down for the last time, I took a light raincoat and went out.

The air seemed to weigh heavily along the unusually sultry streets. The sky was oppressed. I could sense the thunder gathering its forces offstage. There was a feeling of unreality in my mind, as if I were watching a badly produced play. And I was jumpy. I went through the customary doubling-back techniques, half-heartedly searching for a shadow. Whoever it was making the nerves in my back twitch was professional enough to be invisible. For a moment I thought of dodging: only an organised network of radio cars can shadow anybody who doesn't care to be tagged in a crowded city, but I felt too tired and dispirited to go through the motions. It occurred to me as I plodded along that this might even be the right tactic to employ— unless they wanted to kill me, and it's almost ridiculously easy to gun a man in a busy street. People had started to put their raincoats on, the ideal garb for a gunman. I thought that if I were ever really scared I'd spend my days seated on a busy beach in Miami. It's very difficult to conceal a gun or a knife on a beach.

With an effort I dismissed these things from my mind and wandered in and out of a couple of stores before going into the one I really wanted. I bought some clamps and six coach screws, watching the door while the clerk served me. A couple of people came in while I was there, one of them a very large man who peered at a display of automatic tools. When I got my package I hung around window shopping, watching him from the corner of my eye. If he was following me, he was pretty good. Even when I managed to bump into him and apologised, there appeared no tell-tale flicker in his eyes.

Outside the door a cab drew up, discharging its fare. I waited until the driver made change and prepared to drive off, dashed out of the store and opened the door. The cabbie gave me a dirty look and said he had to report back to the depot, I mentioned a double-side tip, and he ground into low gear just as I glimpsed the large man emerging from the store. He walked casually, hands deep in his raincoat pockets, but his face had lost its placidity as he watched the back of the cab.

Back at my apartment building I had a word with the janitor and told him that although I'd give her the usual pay I wouldn't want the cleaning woman inside my apartment next morning. Discretion, built in by the monthly offering of a bottle of bourbon, caused him merely to nod, with just a flavouring of leer on his stolid face.

Upstairs I stood for a minute and eyed my front door. When I moved in I had a new one put on, not obviously different from the others except that it is three-inch weathered timber instead of veneer and junk, its heavy hinges being well set into the wall. I ran a finger-tip over the mortice lock and didn't think it had been worked on. Inside I checked the lock again and slipped home the length of heavy chain that reinforces it. My body felt clammy under the raincoat and I went over and sat for a few minutes on the couch.

The gloom of the dirty sky seemed to seep through the windows into the apartment. I rubbed my finger-tips along the arm of the couch and was surprised when they came away clean.

Presently I got up and checked the apartment, room by room, closet by closet. I didn't really expect to find a bomb, but it was a relief that I didn't. Subtlety I can sometimes deal with. I looked at the kitchen door leading on to the fire escape. Here again, I had had a new door and a new lock. I swung it back and took a magnifying glass, a pair of tweezers and a long sliver of lint. I worked the lint into the key-hole and withdrew it and used the glass. Under the strong magnification appeared shreds of some kind of metal compound. Somebody had taken the impression. I found myself whistling when I went back to the living-room.

I had lived long enough in the place for some of the impersonal apartment-to-rent atmosphere to have rubbed off, or rather to have been replaced by some of the useless, loved impedimenta that an ageing bachelor accumulates. One day I guess I'll have a cat. Meantime a couple of old trout rods, a sea chest of dubious authenticity, a complete donkey harness with Moorish doodads embroidered on it and a pair of shotguns make home for Piron. In my bedroom, with its vast custom-made vehicle for sleeping, brooding and maybe loving, was an old office chair, the last-century mahogany scarred. A modern chair would have collapsed long ago, but my chair still stood, red leather occasionally peeping through the black patina of age, like some old harpy, bowed but still battling after years of intimate embraces. In its creaking clutches, one can swing from side to side, swivel backwards to the groan of rusty springs. But one cannot, when seated, easily move the chair itself, the weight of the wood, the splayed come-what-may stance of the legs, prohibiting such movement. I had paid two dollars for it at auction one rainy day many years ago when, brashly prepared to open my oyster, I had thought it added dignity and strength to my freshly painted office room. All the rest had gone, but somehow I had kept the chair.

I puffed and sweated it into the living-room, placing it a few feet away from the door leading into the kitchen. I got out my purchases and some tools. I saw for what seemed to be the first time that the chair rested upon four sets of mahogany toes, artistically carved and curved. I hoped that the tenant downstairs was out as I ruthlessly anchored two of the wooden feet to the floor with coach screws. The pile of the vandalised carpet was thick enough to hide the heads. I sat down in my old friend and threw my weight around. The chair gasped and groaned, but I couldn't make it tilt or even slightly budge. I have always imagined that it was custom-made originally for a very short and pompous man. A man of six feet has to use his hands to lever himself upwards and out of its voracious clutch.

In front of the chair I placed a large coffee table. It wasn't heavy enough to please me, but I placed two screws through the legs into the floor. A heavy blow would rip the fancy legs in two, but after worrying about it for five minutes or so while I allowed myself one Scotch, I guessed it would do.

Then came the tricky part. I have no aptitude for fancy mechanical stuff, although I did a four-week course on installing microphones, which the Agency paid for. I was officially on holiday, because it is considered very naughty to plant taps on telephones and microphones under beds. And one time an Army sergeant with bad breath had spent a few days trying to improve my capacity to improvise booby-traps.

First I got out an old-fashioned box file. Opening it I carefully pared away the stout cardboard of one wall, so that only the fancy paper on the outside remained.

From the bedroom closet I fished out a small steel box and unlocked it. Just a few mementoes, a fancy belt with a wicked piece of flexible razor-edged steel inside the leather, a rather handy little hypodermic that can masquerade as a leather button, a nicely made apparatus of catgut, throats for the use of, things like that. Most of them I have had occasion to take away from people. What I was looking for could be loosely described as a gun, if you define the term as something which fires a bullet. It was maybe three inches long, designed to be wedged back between the thumb and first finger. There was no barrel, the hand-made cartridge having a wall which projected a couple of inches beyond the end of the soft-lead slug. It was the equivalent of a point-three-two and if you fired it you got a wrenched wrist and bad powder burn : I'd fired it once out of curiosity. It had come to me from a badly scared Syrian who'd hired my watchdog services for a four-day trip into Turkey. As a precaution I had insisted on relieving him of his own little arsenal : one of the main dangers of body-guarding is stopping a bullet fired by the well-meaning client. I remembered that the trip had been uneventful except for unusually bad food and that the client had dropped dead in the small *souk* in Tangier a few months later—from heart failure, everybody said.

I collected one of the three spare cartridges. The chances were that the thing was okay, my client having been so cautious. The powder charge was low, just sufficient to fling the lead at killing velocity for around six feet. Not that you could operate at six feet with reasonable certainty of not missing by four. The general idea was to keep it in your hat and to bring the headgear within six inches of some beloved buddy before pressing a thumb on the activating rod attached to the top of the apparatus.

The thin steel bars with screw holes at each end made a gleaming pile on the table top. If my recent shadow had noted my purchases, I didn't reckon that they could be added up and a correct answer given. I'd told the bored clerk that I was rigging up my own stereophonic set-up. It was a relief to make my mind blank and sweat away with a ruler and the tools, like a child forcing himself to play with a construction set while he waits for his father to spot the broken window.

Eventually I had a little steel nest in which the "gun" rested securely. I reinforced it with twists of thick wire. The last stage was to screw the gun down into the box file, carrying the screws through the veneer table top and down into solid wood underneath. I closed the box and smacked my hand down on top of it, and heard the instantaneous click of the firing-pin. I recocked it and repeated the action, with the same result. Gingerly I inserted the cartridge, made a final cautious adjustment, and closed the lid. It was rather like setting a mousetrap. However he—or she—twisted in that chair the flying lead would hit somewhere around the navel. Soft-lead being what it is, the score would be a cavity roughly the size of an orange.

The rest was waiting, at which I have had practice. I had no idea how long. The room grew dark and I drew the drapes. I carefully arranged a pen and bundles of paper on the table top and brought in a light kitchen chair. Under my coat I put on a spring shoulder-holster with a standard point three-eight. It showed. They always do unless you have a doctored model, which probably is not accurate, or a small gun, requiring Annie Oakley proficiency. I considered the inner man and settled for the Scotch bottle, a holder filled with ice, and a copy of a collection of comic verse. Behind my chair I arranged a lamp which would shine over my right shoulder quite naturally. I settled down, limiting myself to one very small Scotch per hour. The comic verse didn't seem comic as I ploughed on. Three times the telephone rang. I made myself ignore it. Time had run out. It was too late. The rain beat solidly against the windows.

The chimes on the doorbell were chosen for softness, but my hands jerked up in nervous reaction when they came. I told myself to take it steady, just as a trapped rat might tell himself. I forced myself to walk to the door and peer through the spyhole.

It was just at the right height to give me a close-up of Gretyl Siskin's face. I found myself noticing that the haggardness of the skin merely accentuated the beauty of the bones underneath. I froze there, my head turned to watch the kitchen door. The chimes rang out again and I disengaged the chain, opened the door and told her to come in.

I tucked myself well behind the door as I opened it, and closed it so swiftly that it knocked her in passing. I heard her exhalation of annoyance as I re-engaged the chain.

Her eyes were angry, somehow reflecting the brilliance of her eyes.

"Well, what is it?" The voice was low and unkind.

I looked at her, and paused a second. I knew I had no time to get things wrong.

"I haven't communicated with you for three days."

Her eyes narrowed. "You're up to something. You phoned an hour ago about some papers of Harry's I should have."

"Gretyl," I said gently, "now you're to do what I say. I swear to God that otherwise I'll knock you out and tie you up."

She was not the kind of woman who likes that kind of thing. I could see her stiffen and her eyes flicker round the room. I caught hold of a chair and rammed it back against the wall at the side of the front door.

"Just sit there," I said. "Sit there quiet and if you ever had any time for me, for God's sake stay still and stay silent."

I was surprised when she obeyed. I should take on taming lions.

Resuming my position behind the coffee-table I saw that she was in shadow beyond the range of the lamp. A few seconds of time shuffled past.

She started to speak. "Piron, you must be mad."

"Just very scared."

She was an intelligent woman, thank God. One could feel her mind registering.

She started to say something and stopped. After that we waited together. I saw the clock hands erase one minute softly. In the distance, thunder pealed.

My mind suddenly became very clear as I saw the door to the kitchen start to move very slowly open. I had been watching a jumbled, jerky cinema film. Now it was as if one of the frames had frozen, close-up, on the screen.

Before the door opened sufficiently for me to see him, I said, "Come in, Mr. Pout. I thought you'd be earlier."

The tricky lighting further confused him. He stood for a moment, filling the doorway with his bulk, the rain from his felt hat and dark raincoat dripping on the carpet. I couldn't see his face. His gloved hands were clasped across his stomach.

"Sit down, man, and relax."

Almost mechanically he came forward and sat in my old office chair. As he felt the springs give under his weight, realisation must have hit him. He'd made a mistake, and in the Big Game it's not always the end moves that count, so much as the early ones. The rest is liable to follow inevitably.

Like the seasoned campaigner he was, he just sat there, getting his eyes accustomed to the light. I heard his carefully controlled breathing and saw him force his muscles to relax. Carefully he reached out and placed his sodden hat on the floor. His face had aged ten years since I had last seen him and the smooth flesh had fallen into hollows under the prominent cheekbones.

His white teeth showed in a line between taut lips. I thought that a man would probably look like this lying behind a hide-out in some stinking jungle awaiting the arrival of a tiger. Raindrops looked like little beads of perspiration beside his nose.

He carefully tested the chair, found it immovable, and then twisted sideways, squinting his eyes. Finally he found Gretyl, and I heard a soft exhalation of breath. He turned to face me, hands still clasped. So tense had I been that I had forgotten the thunder. Now it came again, more softly, a roll of drums in the distance.

His raincoat was loose upon him and the sleeves looked very wide. I guessed he had a gun strapped against one forearm, the fastest way of drawing it if you can wear the necessary camouflage. Colour had come back into his cheeks. He'd have looked up my record. I'm slowish with a gun. I guessed Pout would be very fast, some of the security lads are.

I sat forward and placed my hands on the tabletop. He gave me a long look between slitted lids and turned to both sides and methodically surveyed the room.

I said: "You're about at the end of your tether, Pout,

and you're a gambler. That's a worrying combination."

His big, well-manicured hand took a cigarette from the open box on the table. It didn't tremble when he reached for the lighter, his clever blue eyes now smiling over the thin stream of smoke. He inhaled very deeply.

"It must have been quite hell waiting until now," I observed.

"Piron," he said, "I think you're a little out of your mind." His nice, mellow voice could have been discussing the weather.

This was going to be bad. I felt like banging the box file right away. If there hadn't been a witness, I guess I would have.

"Sure," I said. "I always find it difficult to stay put in it. I sort of jump out, like when I got to realising that the best spy is the guy who is employed by a very specialised, comparatively unimportant department engaged in anti-espionage. He has access to a lot of things: the activities are so obscure that other agencies in the business aren't supposed to know what goes on."

He laughed aloud, his teeth gleaming in the light. I had a nasty thought about power failures. He was a man I would not like to play tag with in the dark. I watched as he swivelled the seat slightly so that a movement of his head would transfer his line of vision from me to Gretyl. I kept my eyes rigidly on his face. If you concentrate enough it is remarkable what a range of vision the human eye has. As well as his face, I could see his hands, the cigarettes held lightly in the left, the right finger-tips a few inches from the left sleeve. In the background I was conscious of Gretyl sitting rigidly on the edge of her chair. Her skirt had rucked up so that I could see her thighs. Pressure had pushed fat and muscle over to one side so that she looked painfully thin unless, as I did, you knew better. A tremor of shock ate into my mind as I saw that she had a wallet on her lap. I couldn't be certain but I thought it was fastened. I remembered the gun I had given her and prayed she hadn't brought it along.

I kept talking fast, not daring to lose the initiative. "I poked around and found that you had lost your money. The family business goes on, but you aren't connected with it. The last male Pout except you lost his money in the Depression. You had a fair income from your mother's estate but with post-war taxes it didn't stretch quite far enough for your tastes. So you gambled, very discreetly. So did a lot of guys. In uranium. It looked smart at the time, only there proved to be too much of the stuff and your concessions weren't rich enough to pay. You couldn't take it."

The hand holding the cigarette jerked once, twice, and then held still by conscious effort. He reached out and stubbed it. Only a professional could know the art and training behind his smile. "I don't know what kind of frame-up this is, Piron, but I'll give you all the rope you want."

It was my turn to smirk. "Wondering whether I've planted a bug? Or whether I've got a couple of men in the bedroom? Wonder on, friend Pout."

Here was a bit of safe ground and he couldn't resist it, although with his training he should have kept quiet.

"I've had a good look at you, Jim," he said. "I don't think you'd be recording this, old boy. For one thing your Boss wouldn't touch a crazy caper like this. For another, you're the Great Piron, the original egotistical little private rat."

The Big Game was proceeding as it always does. He'd lost the first few moves, but had consolidated a nice defence. Perhaps he was a bit nervous. It was my cue to fiddle with my big pieces.

"I'm glad you smiled when you said that, Pout. Just for the record, you can't make me mad at you, not tonight. As I was saying, one of the guys that got burned with you was Marcello, operating through his Social Investments. It's on record, if anyone likes to dig.

"I guess you thought it over and decided to utilise the contact. You knew enough to tell Marcello the right people to approach, and the whole kernel of the thing was money. It takes money, lots of it, to finance espionage and, of course, they try to avoid bringing the greenstuff in through official channels. Marcello couldn't keep away from crooked deals.

"There were other things. I telephoned Professor Dwyer and asked him what the letters G.L. in that bit of a diary Harry Siskin left could possibly mean. He put forward dozens of ideas : he's an ingenious old fellow."

Pout showed polite interest, an eyebrow raised, head slightly bowed. I felt like I did once in World War II when we were going through a deserted village looking for booby-traps.

"I had an idea . . ."

He gave me another glimpse of his teeth. "You have the goddamnedest ideas, Piron."

". . . an idea. The day he died, Siskin had jumped down the throat of a fellow who joshed him. I phoned up and asked what the joke was. It had been connected with his apparent lack of ambition. Somebody made a remark about him preferring to associate with small fish. So I asked the Prof to pay particular attention to fish allusions, which shortened a long job." I moved my hand very slowly and took a cigarette. I could hear Gretyl's breathing in the silence.

"The answer was *Gadus luscus*, the name given to a fish commonly known as Pout. It seemed interesting. Marcello used the fish motif. But I didn't think it referred to him."

Although now the moisture on his wide forehead was sweat and not rain, his broad chest heaved and his blue eyes sparkled as he hooted with laughter. Only the fact that his hands did not shift from their careful arrangement betrayed the fake.

I glanced at the little desk clock. The hands had shoved forward suddenly to one, the hour of suicides.

I swore aloud at the simplicity of the thing. "We'll try to make it short, Mr. Pout. I made phone calls. I have a few friends. After pulling a lot of teeth I got the fact that the capsule our mutual friend Mr. Brown told us about—the one the workmen found—could have been a few years old. It's true the information is still top classification, but it could have gone right back to the time the old Colonel was operating. The rest of the stuff, a suicide, something coming back from a neutral country—phooey. You know what I thought?"

His lips were pursed and he looked as though he was whistling and thinking about something else.

"I'll tell you free, my friend. You can't keep some new espionage development completely secret. In Berlin there's a whole market in rumours. It got about that something new is happening in good old New York. So you played it down, confused it, invented a new spymaster paid by Red China. Anything to keep the word 'money' out of it. But somehow the name of Marcello came on the file.

"That was where Siskin came in. He'd gotten neurotic. Apart from the tendency of the job to produce ulcers, Harry, who was a highly intelligent guy, couldn't understand why he was constantly being lifted off the scent just when he thought he might be getting somewhere. He brooded and did a little work on his own. This was the Sybil Green dame. You contacted Marcello about the time she split up with him. Maybe she had seen you with him. When she'd sobered up she'd tell Marcello, or maybe spit it at him when she was drunk. So Harry had to go."

The half-smile still persisted from habit, but it had become a terrible thing.

"I've had enough of this." His voice was almost a whisper, but there was the underlying morbid curiosity that I have heard at other times. The muscles of his face were set in the smiling picture, but the upper lip had curled up and deep down in his eyes were tiny pinpoints of hate. I watched his hands. Gretyl had opened the wallet with a snap and I knew he had heard it, too.

There was still a little time left. I continued. "You told me how you collared an enemy agent in a Berlin hotel. That would be five years ago. I telephoned a friend to check on what was the favourite lethal weapon then. It was a pistol holding very small pellets and operated by compressed air. The pellet entered the skin so fast that it left no mark on the skin. It snapped back with an elastic effect. When they struck bone, the pellets disintegrated. They were, of course, toxic and produced the effect of cyanide poisoning. Verdict, suicide. Today they're using something else."

He had regained his control now: the smile was normal, the muscles relaxed.

"I'll do you the favour, Piron, of putting down this little exercise in fiction as a joke. You haven't introduced me to the lady, by the way."

I wagged my head, "I admire you, Pout. I really do. It was so easy for you to put an agent, another guy like Siskin, to follow me today, but suppose you hadn't summed me up right and I'd gone to my Boss. Every hour you'd be waiting to be picked up."

I pressed the attack home, feeling little beads of sweat under my chin. "You know, Pout, you're a perfectionist, you told me so. I could have told you that this desire is the worst thing for a killer to have. They are usually caught if they try to cobble up all the loose ends. What you hoped was that Mrs. Siskin would be booked on a murder charge. Things didn't work out that way, and then I came along. Nosy, a snooper like you said. And I was getting near to Mrs. Green."

His eyes showed he wasn't liking it, not one bit.

"It was a devil of a fix. You couldn't kill the Green woman because of what she had on Marcello. So you started to play it by ear. You got Marcello back from Las Vegas and frightened him into setting a murder trap for me. I don't think Marcello killed his girl friend. I think you did that. You would have arranged to see him at the apartment. When he returned you'd panic him, tell him he'd been framed. He'd take the money and stones from his safe and run. Or alternatively you might have killed him. But he didn't come back."

He managed a yawn and deliberately picked up his hat. There was a hateful knowing quality in his face. I'd failed to win the Big Game. At best it was a draw.

A thunderous knock shook the front door. A nervous tic contorted my left cheek. His nerves were better than mine. He sat as though carved from granite.

"Open up, the law here." The voice, a bronchial basso, could belong to no one else but a vintage New York cop.

I felt rather than saw him tense.

I saw his thoughts chase through his now expressive face. The time factor, the chance of a last successful bluff, were being computed. The door shivered as shoulders crashed against it. For once I cursed its stoutness and reinforcing.

His hand began to move. His right hand had snaked inside his sleeve by the time I slapped the top of the box file. The explosion seemed very loud and his coat front blossomed horribly as the impact tilted the heavy chair on its springs.

There was another crash on the door as I ran round the desk. I bent swiftly and saw the blue eyes glaze. There was blood on his lips as he mumbled, "Right, only money. Hate . . . bastards," and died.

The cream of the jest had suddenly struck me. I was sorry that I couldn't tell it to him. He was a considerable man, was Pout. I like to think he would have enjoyed it.

The gun I had given Gretyl was in her hand. She looked bemused, half tearful, half resentful, like a small child at her first party. I paused to take it off her and put it in my pocket. The noise from the door was fearful.

I shouted, "Officer, I will open up." The noise ceased.

Cops and cops and cops, may the Lord love them! Feet sore and flattened on the concrete, brain conditioned by the fears and sneers and furtive looks. Night school for the ambitious, the bullet in the belly for the unlucky. Sometimes a calloused mind, and who would blame the man?

By the time I got the door open, fingers fumbling with the chain, the assault had begun again. The leader, who strained out of his uniform and would probably have strained out of any size uniform, tumbled past me and nearly fell as I braced myself against the flying door.

He was built like a sturdy packing case on legs, black eyes snapping from creased leathery skin. Beyond him was a younger man, his considerable weight above his waist, blue eyes in slightly less leathery skin. Most plainclothesmen are on the pasty side. I always think selection boards operate entirely on skin effects : leathery equates with motor cycles, prowl cars and the beat.

They had their guns out. I turned and let one frisk me. He grunted at the guns and looked in Gretyl's handbag.

She sat there like an outsize doll, her eyes puckered.

The young one swore as he briefly looked at Pout's body. "Dead meat here." He looked in the other rooms.

The older guy jerked his hand towards Gretyl. "Your wife or his?"

"Neither," I said, "widdy woman."

"Don't be smart, mister, for your own good." He wasn't unfriendly.

"There's a doctor living here, 207, second floor," I told them. The younger one departed, the older man standing where he could keep his Police Positive well focused on me.

"I want to telephone Inspector McMurdo. My name's Piron. I was at the funeral today."

Something flickered behind his hard black eyes. So you are a harness bull, grinding along the streets, no promotion this side of the pension. The book says leave homicide to the specialists, play everything by that rule book, and the wages come in safely. Yet there is always ambition. A stroke beyond the call of duty, a notation that superior intelligence has been displayed and some promotion comes, to be weighed in terms of pension and maybe a little block in Florida. It's a gamble, with a transfer to the end of nowhere as the loser's end.

After he had taken a good look at me, I said : "He'll probably be off duty. Let me speak to the guy who's on."

I went slowly towards the telephone and picked it up. I dialled H.Q. homicide. He didn't interfere.

I got through to a lieutenant. "My name's Piron. The Marcello one. I've got a dead man in my apartment, plus two officers from the beat. I want to talk to McMurdo."

There was a long silence. The lieutenant was thinking hard. In this way we make the decision that may lead up or down.

Finally he said with admirable caution: "Mr. Piron, the Inspector's at home, probably asleep. First I'd like you to hang up so that I can check on your private number. Then I'll see."

I replaced the receiver. "Calling me back," I told the big cop.

The call came through. He still sounded cautious, but told me to hang on. After a minute or so McMurdo came through, thickly, like a man aroused from heavy sleep.

"I've just killed Pout," I said, and waited for his reaction.

"For God's sake! Are you crazy?"

"No kidding. I'd like you to come to the apartment."

"This isn't my business, Piron. I'm off duty."

I flung the bait. "Smart boys get sugar plums, McMurdo."

"Eh?"

I repeated it. He'd heard the first time. I heard his heavy breathing and then he started to swear. He wasn't a foul-mouthed man, rather the cold executive, but in his profession you pick up some interesting turns of expression. I heard a female squawk. Mrs. McMurdo had awakened and was protesting against such terms in the nuptial bed.

He'd assessed it and in spite of his language couldn't miss the chance. Perhaps a deputy-commissionership if he played it right. He swore like a man whose life's objective gets changed around two a.m.

"I can't come alone, Piron," he said. "Can't take that risk."

"Bring a couple of young, discreet kids who're ambitious."

I hung up. The cop had let his gun dangle at his side. He'd caught enough to sense promotion in the offing. The other man came back with the doctor, trousers under a pyjama coat. I knew him vaguely by sight as I caught his curious stare. He gave a couple of seconds to Pout and shrugged.

Gretyl had started to shake. Silent, racking hiccoughs, arms wrapped round her breasts.

He looked at her and put his hand on her forehead.

"Near shock," he said, looking at me.

"Bedroom's over there, Doctor. Perhaps you could get her in and give her a mild sedative, nothing that would put her out completely."

He nodded and caught her up from the chair in a professional hoist. I sat down on the couch and closed my eyes. Presently I heard him leave. The two cops were muttering together in basso rumbles.

It took McMurdo forty minutes to get to the apartment. His whipcord body was slightly bent with fatigue. With him were a couple of smartly dressed young plainclothesmen around thirty, the age where a man needs a break. McMurdo's shirt was unbuttoned to reveal greying hair and his suit coat didn't match the pants. Nevertheless he didn't forget carefully to enquire the names of the two cops and to ask them courteously to wait outside. "Guard the door," was his phrase.

He looked at Pout distastefully. I told him Gretyl was in the bedroom and he checked.

He squatted on the couch. The two plainclothesmen stood, trying to look impassive.

"Okay, give it quick." He looked at the other two. "This is confidential. Get over the other side of the room. But I want you to record anything I take or touch."

"One minute," I said. "Would you detail one of them for an errand? I want him to look into every all-night bar, alley, the all-night drug-stores and quick snack counters, for a block around and memorise faces."

Without looking pleased he told one of the men to do that. The other one stood with his back against the door.

"Have a look at Pout," I told him. "Sleeve gun and I'd guess an envelope in his breast pocket."

He peered into the blood-sodden mess of Pout's left coat-sleeve and sighed. Taking out a handkerchief to cover his hand he dipped briefly under the raincoat and into the inside jacket pocket of the suit-coat. He came out with a square envelope.

"I guess that would be my suicide note," I said.

He rummaged in his old jacket and got out a wallet. He selected a pair of serrated rubber finger-tips, of the type used for counting money. The envelope, marked "Coroner", wasn't sealed. He prised up the flap and using his covered forefinger and second finger drew out a folded sheet of paper.

"There won't be any fingerprints," I said. "They'd have gone on afterwards."

It was a plain statement to say that Gretyl and I had decided on a suicide pact. We would take poison. Both our signatures were there. I couldn't vouch for hers, but mine looked genuine.

"I think I recognise the typewriter face," I said, keeping my voice down. "A battered old thing I use around here. And the stationery's mine."

He put the letter back on the table and jerked his eyebrows.

I said, rapidly, "Pout was a naughty boy. He was scared Mrs. Siskin would remember something; scared that I would stumble over a discrepancy. He set Marcello on me."

McMurdo bit his thin lower lip.

"I don't like it, Piron. This is for the Coroner. If other departments want to take over, okay by me."

"But suppose it isn't quite like that?"

I looked at him for a long second and suggested he take a further look at the corpse. He got down on one knee and gingerly explored. There was a wallet, the gun, which took him five minutes to extract, and a small green bottle.

"Take a look at the gun first," I suggested.

It was stubby in a square holster which he had unstrapped from Pout's wrist.

He peered at it cautiously. "Compressed air," he grunted.

"That's odd. Looks like a high-velocity job, but take a look at the muzzle—too small unless you punctured the brain."

"But the slugs have got a concentrated mixture of cyanide inside. You just hit a bone, the skin snaps back after the slug, and you're cyanosed to hell. Now look at that bottle. I'd bet a year's pay that's ordinary chemist's cyanide. That's how the double suicide was to be staged. He was unlucky."

His face was sour with distaste. Before he could sort out any words, the elderly uniformed man came in with exaggerated discretion wrinkled over his face.

"There's a man," he began, when the tiny figure of Mr. Brown brushed past him. The verb is exact although perhaps seven stone separated their weights. It said a lot for the little man's presence that the cop discreetly withdrew, like a fifteen-stone wraith.

The apple face was as unpleasing in expression as I remembered it. Its glance went over and past me.

"Inspector!" Brown held out a small bound book, like a passport except that the cover was grey.

McMurdo flipped it open, dwelt for a few seconds to settle his mind, and got up. He ordered the plainclothesman outside.

Mr. Brown stared momentarily at Pout, his expression unchanging.

"This matter, Inspector," he said, "concerns me only in that I shall take charge of all private documents in the corpse's possession. This includes any at his home."

"We had a look at the suicide note. My suicide note!" I put it in to give McMurdo time to think. His glare towards me had thoughts in it that I didn't like.

Brown's glacial eyes flickered at my face. "This man had some personal enmity towards Pout, which I must admit was reciprocated. A woman, I believe. I have no doubt this resulted from a brawl." He looked pointedly at my bottle of whisky.

"That's for the Coroner," muttered McMurdo.

"For the moment," said Brown, "hold this man incommunicado. In an hour or so your superiors will get a directive."

I think McMurdo was prepared to call it a day, to put the departmental wheels into operation, to chuck responsibility to the Coroner and to "upstairs". But the door opened again, and the fresh-faced plainclothesman we had sent out around the block came in.

"I want no disturbance," said Mr. Brown, his words like the slap of wet fish on a marble slab. It was a mistake. It roused something in McMurdo. In any case, the youngster was staring at Brown.

"Recognise anybody?" I said quickly.

"Yes, sir. This gentleman was seated in the all-night drug store. I saw him leave six minutes ago."

"Have a look at his shoes," I invited McMurdo.

Brown glanced down and tried to shuffle his feet. It was a mistake for such a small man. He lost face. The once-shiny brown surface of the expensive leather was discoloured and sodden. It takes a lot of exposure to rain to do that.

I saw McMurdo's jaw muscles tighten. He told the plainclothesman to wait outside.

Mr. Brown watched us, his pale blue eyes unwavering. You could never change him or break him. My job was over. I saw McMurdo's worldly-wise face tighten. This was his ground.

"Mr. Brown, how did you know it had occurred?" His voice was suave, a little tired.

"That is my business." The voice was cold, ruthless, but a little of the authority had gone from it.

McMurdo reached over to the handset and dialled. He fired questions while Brown remained standing, hardly moving a muscle.

The Inspector replaced the handset and said, "Mr. Brown, a man tipped off the local precinct house at one fifteen that there was a dangerous disturbance here."

"And there, Inspector," said Brown, "you get on to ground which is not your concern."

McMurdo rubbed his jaw. His eyes sought mine, this time as a friend.

I said: "You know, McMurdo, after the Marcello business I couldn't face any kind of jury. Where would I be? I might have settled for a plea of manslaughter and maybe two years.

"So as it is, my Boss would spend the money to find that Mr. Brown has been hanging around this apartment for two hours. Don't worry, he'd do that come high water." I tried to sound completely sure.

"Inspector, take this man into custody!"

In the higher forms of life, such as espionage, perhaps one loses the common touch. In McMurdo's eyes was the certainty of promotion. He merely said, in an accent he probably hadn't used for thirty years, "Shaddup!"

"Mr. McMurdo isn't Pentagon, isn't even Washington, sir," I rubbed in saltily. "Let me put it straight. Mrs. Siskin was a tethered goat, so I thought, stupidly. But I was the goat. Just lucky enough to worry Pout, whom you suspected."

"You're in shock, Piron. Inspector . . ."

I interrupted him with a word that brought him a step nearer me. Even at the weights, I would rather have tangled with a rattlesnake than him.

"Pout was double-crossing you, sir. You aren't a fool and Pout was very much the egotist. You have a department that has been under fire. You can't afford to have such a scandal. While Pout was shadowing me or causing me to be shadowed, you were the third man. The general idea was that Pout would commit murder and be taken red-handed. It would be an open-and-shut case with no political angle admissible.

"On the other hand, if I killed Pout, I'd have to be a good boy and plead manslaughter. You followed Pout, and after a bit you realised that it was not going well. In fact Pout had decided not to go through with it. My guess is that he would have decided to bluff it out—my case was pretty thin. Or else he could have run for it, he was a resourceful fellow. So you put through the call to the police earlier than you intended. You knew Pout well. When that knocking came at the door he gambled. It's a stout door. It could have held long enough for him to kill two people, put the suicide note, spill some cyanide into two glasses and get out through the kitchen."

Brown's apple-face creased for a moment.

"Inspector," he said, "this man is talking nonsense. I think that perhaps you and I should make a few telephone calls. No doubt you'll co-operate."

McMurdo became very professional. "We're always pleased to co-operate with other services in confidential political matters, sir."

It was over. The treaty was made. He had adroitly manoeuvred Brown on to the spot. For McMurdo compliments for discretion and a big entry on the credit side.

"I don't think you want me here."

McMurdo scratched his nose. "I guess I'd better send you along to headquarters." He was apologetic.

I shook my head. "It's nothing to do with me, McMurdo. If Pout wanted to commit suicide in his own apartment, what is it to me except money for a wreath?"

As far as Brown was concerned I wasn't in the room.

The more he thought about it, the less McMurdo wanted me hanging around at headquarters or the nearest precinct house until he'd cleared the details.

"Okay," he said. "Only one thing. Phone me in a couple of hours' time. I'll probably be here: if not leave a message at my office."

"I'll drop Mrs. Siskin home." I addressed the ceiling over Brown's head. "She's had a bad time. Maybe a visit could be arranged from somebody to tell her that Siskin died in the line of duty."

He hadn't replied by the time I got to the bedroom. Gretyl was curled on my bed, half propped against the piled pillows, her feet curled up under her skirt. She had been crying a little.

"Feel like going home?"

She swung her legs onto the floor. I helped her up.

"Feel dopey?"

She shook her head. "I'm all right, a little dizzy."

I collected her wallet and felt her weight on my arm as I took her to the front door. McMurdo opened it and told the older of the uniformed men that it was okay.

I couldn't resist saying "Thanks, sergeant" to the leather-faced old cop. McMurdo started to look annoyed, but it came out as a grin. The cop kept at attention, but for a split second one eyelid dropped slightly as he stared over my head.

The hackie was pimpled and bored. He drove up as I held her, the sour sweetness of old fear upon us both. In the cab she dropped against me. I had to ask her for the new address.

Me and my girl jolted through the night to the concrete impersonality of her new apartment. She stirred. I fumbled for money.

Stiffly, wearily she got out of the door I had opened for her. She looked at me as if she were looking for the first time.

"I should say thank you." I watched her as she turned away, her fingers already prying in the opened wallet for the bright new key. The outer door closed behind her.

"If it's waiting time you want..." the hackie's voice was a dentist's drill.

"I want the nearest telephone, friend Kinsey."

I thought of the Countess, my pen-pal, as I lounged in the smoky recesses of my private pony express. I reached for my wallet and her photograph and telephone number. Then I remembered that both reposed on the night table beside my bed.

I rapped and yelled to the driver and gave him the address of a modest hotel where I have a credit rating.

*If you have enjoyed this book, you might
wish to join the Walker British Mystery Society.*

*For information, please send a postcard or
letter to:*

Paperback Mystery Editor

**Walker & Company
720 Fifth Avenue
New York, NY 10019**